HELL HAD NO FURY

"Well," said Mrs. Barrow, "you finally woke up. This is the third time I've come down to welcome you. Even squeezed your pecker, but it didn't even make you breathe hard. The Reverend Philip must have laid it on you good."

"I think I hit the door on the way down," I told her.

"We've been checking you out," she said. "Newspapers say you're the detective looking into the killing of that gook used-car dealer. Why'd you come sniffing around our church?"

"My wife died," I said, "and this policeman I work with told me that—"

She pulled the gun from the holster. I watched her face as she did it, and there was the tiniest hint of a smile just before the blackness wiped her and everything else out. It was as if she had come with the intention of whacking me with her gun, and things had gone just the way she had hoped.

Which wasn't exactly the way things were going for me. . . .

D1440878

THE MOVING FINGER

MILTON BASS

A SIGNET BOOK

NEW AMERICAN LIBRARY

NAL BOOKS ARE AVAILABLE AT QUANTITY DISCOUNTS WHEN USED TO
PROMOTE PRODUCTS OR SERVICES. FOR INFORMATION PLEASE WRITE
TO PREMIUM MARKETING DIVISION, NEW AMERICAN LIBRARY,
1633 BROADWAY, NEW YORK, NEW YORK 10019.

 SIGNET TRADEMARK REG. U.S. PAT. OFF. AND FOREIGN COUNTRIES
REGISTERED TRADEMARK—MARCA REGISTRADA
HECHO EN CHICAGO, U.S.A.

SIGNET, SIGNET CLASSIC, MENTOR, PLUME, MERIDIAN
and NAL BOOKS
are published by New American Library,
1633 Broadway, New York, New York 10019

First Printing, February, 1986

1 2 3 4 5 6 7 8 9

PRINTED IN THE UNITED STATES OF AMERICA

For Amy Bass and Kosy Kid:
One a wag, the other a wagger

1

Some nights I could swear I'd never slept a wink, eyes open and staring at the ceiling, listening to her push each breath out and pull another one in, never sure that the next one was going to come, either out or in, and my guts would tighten up until I had to do it her way too, out and in, out and in, until we were one, and I could feel the pain too, out and in, out and in, out and in.

That was how it first hit me that she was dead, that she wasn't there anymore. I was doing it alone. Eyes wide open, staring at the ceiling. Out and in, out and in, out and in. It was just me. Alone. Once again in my life I was all alone. And I opened my mouth and screamed at the ceiling, screamed and screamed with no sound coming out, like a painting I had seen somewhere of souls tormented in hell. And that's where I was in the thirty-third year of my life, right straight in hell.

I had taken the phone out of the bedroom three weeks before when I brought her home from the hospital, so I slid out of bed and went into the kitchen. I tried looking at her as I went by the foot of the bed, but my head wouldn't turn. It was like looking at a skeleton with a thin, waxy paste glistening on the bones, the skin stretched over the face so tight that she always seemed to have a little smile on her lips. But she wasn't smiling. The pain cut through all the dope that was being dripped into her and took away all smiles. And now my laughing girl was never going to smile again.

Doc answered on the second ring. His grunt was like the small woof of a dog that isn't sure he knows you, a warning that there could be a bite as well as a wag.

"She's gone," I told him.

"Get some clothes on," he instructed. "I'll be there in thirty-five minutes. The people from the funeral home will be there in an hour. Whatever you want to say to her while there's just the two of you, get it done while you've got time."

I shaved before I put my clothes on, picking each item as though I was already on my way to the funeral. The digital clock said it was 3:40 A.M. and that special thick San Diego fog outside the window almost made a sound as it tried to poke its way through the glass, smelling death and wanting to be part of it. I kept walking around the room without being able to look at her, moving my head and my body at just the right angle to see only walls and furniture and clothes. There was nothing more to say; I'd said it all those days and nights I had sat by her chair and then her bed, going over the three great months when we'd gotten to know each other and then the first five months of our marriage. We didn't say a word about the four months after that. The doctors did all the talking. And now the funeral people that Doc had contacted would finish it up. All finished.

I could feel something growing inside my body, trying to push up from my stomach through the throat into my head, where it would push and push until the skull wouldn't take it anymore, and I would explode into a million pieces with little sticks of bone flying all over the room.

I fell forward onto the floor and started pumping my arms, up and down, up and down, up and down, just the way her chest had heaved as she'd tried to suck in the air, until finally there was no strength left and I collapsed on the rug, my face buried in the thick, harsh nylon. But the pressure was gone; I could gasp; I could breathe.

And I could also finally look at her.

"What about me?" I asked her. "What happens to me?"

All that I got was that little smile on her face, the kind of smile that had reflected back at me from everybody else before I met her. She was gone. Forever. Once again I was all alone.

2

Just like always, he made believe he didn't know I was standing there in front of his desk, but this time, for the first time, I wanted to reach down and pull hard on the bristly hairs sticking out of his nose, hard enough to find out if there were any brains that might come with them.

It wasn't that he was singling me out from the pack; he was like that famous football coach who treated everybody the same—like dogs. Usually I waited him out, analyzing the various parts of his body from the broken veins in his purple nose to the dirt you knew had to be sitting in the soft flesh pockets between his toes. And then he'd look up as if he'd been thinking about something important, which you were interrupting, and growl some obscenity to make sure you got the point.

But I was still out of kilter from Cathy falling off the end of the world, and not in the mood for the games people play to build their little egos into whatever they need to live by.

"Captain," I said softly, and he made believe he didn't hear me. My hand was moving toward his nose before I knew it was on the loose, and the strain of changing its direction to land on his shoulder instead broke a film of sweat on my forehead. There must also have been some kind of expression on my face because when he looked up, he swallowed whatever filth he was about to pour out and just stared at me like I was something from outer space.

"Benny," he finally managed. "What the hell are you doing here?"

"I'm reporting for duty."

"But you're on leave. Your wife . . ."

"I buried her yesterday," I told him.

"Oh yeah. Oh yeah. I was planning to go but . . ."

"We got her in all right," I said.

"But you're . . ."

"I straightened everything out at headquarters, Captain. I'm reporting for duty. My leave is over and I'm reporting for assignment."

He shuffled through the papers on his desk, pursing his fat lips like a hooker who was about to do something with her mouth that wasn't in the ordinary bill of fare. I really didn't like this man. For two years I had watched him screw up cases and policemen's lives, and one night I had gone so far in my mind as to seriously consider fragging him out. He had to have been some kind of cop sometime because even with connections you don't get to be a captain of homicide in a city as busy at it as this one. But booze and a high-cholesterol diet had squeezed out whatever white cells had run his show in the good days, and now he was something to contend with or bypass, whichever worked better at that particular moment.

"You're not working with Morales no more," he said. "His transfer to helicopter came through."

"He told me at the funeral yesterday. All my friends were there."

"Yeah. Okay, let's see what we got. The Dienben case. Moran's been getting nowhere with that. Yes sir, that's what we'll do. You're assigned to the Dienben case. You'll work alone until you develop some leads and then we'll take it from there. Moran can brief you on what he's developed, which should take all of ten seconds. And then you can take it from there. And then next week we'll put it in the dead file."

He dropped his head again and resumed staring at the papers. The man could sit in that position for hours. Everybody was good at something.

Moran wasn't anywhere to be found so I dropped down to the morgue to see if Doc was in. He was soaking his hands in the sink that was filled with a dark, bubbly solution, and staring into the mirror above it.

"You know," he said, "I've been taking stiffs apart for some thirty-five years and I've never touched one part of one without wearing rubber gloves. Yet my hands never feel clean. Sometimes when I'm being intimate with my wife, I suddenly pull my hands off her, straight up in the air, and she says, 'What's the matter? What's the matter?', and I've never been able to tell her what's the matter. I don't know what's the matter. And I have a feeling I don't really want to know what's the matter. How are you doing?"

"I'm officially back at work. The captain gave me a case that Moran's been working on, but he's not around so I guess I'll try to dig up some files."

"Which one is it?"

"He said Dienben."

"Ah," said Doc, "welcome home. Troo Song Dienben, pronounced Dee-en-ben, forty-nine-year-old Vietnamese refugee with successful used-car business. Found a little over a month ago in the passenger seat of a 1981 Toyota sedan, in excellent condition, I might add, the car, not Troo, strangled by a commando-type wire that almost severed the head from the body. One of the interesting facets of the case was that the right index finger had been severed with what we estimated to be a bolt cutter and placed neatly in a plastic sandwich bag on the driver's seat. You obviously read no papers while Cathy was sick because it was plastered all over the front pages. If you give the finger to this city, the city responds in kind."

"All dead ends, I take it."

"If you're not making a pun, I take it too, because I haven't heard a word about what was happening for at least two weeks. I didn't even know that Moran had it as his baby."

"It's my baby now."

"And may it grow into an adult that will make you proud. I think you're smart going right back to work."

"I don't want to think about me right now, Doc. I want to work twenty-four hours a day seven days a week. I do want to thank you for all you did. You're a pretty special person and I don't think I could have managed without your help. The other doctors—"

"Hey, Benny," he broke in. "You're the pretty special person. You've always been a loner and I didn't know you that well before all this, but any man who would marry a woman in that stage of cancer . . ."

He could tell by the look on my face that something was wrong and that it had to do with what he had said. Doc never pushed anything. He waited.

"She didn't have cancer when we got married," I told him. "The cancer came afterward."

When you've done as many interrogations as I have, you get to know people's bodies as a whole. You don't just watch their faces or their eyes or how stiff their shoulders are. Just a blink, or one ear getting redder than the other, or a wrinkle on the forehead is enough to put you on the alert, to tie together what is going through the mind and the body at the same time. Doc was putting it all together for himself, deciding what was best for me in the long run. He knew I knew what he was doing, but it was his decision, and all I could do was wait him out.

"She knew about that cancer last year, Benny. She knew about it six months before you got married. Dr. Allen made the first diagnosis. All the doctors figured you knew. We all figured you had to know. Christ, she never even told you? Nothing? Not a hint? She never even gave you a choice? Where the hell did you meet her?"

"At Carlos Murphy's in Old Town. It was the night I shot that guy in the shoulder during the liquor-store stakeout. I was too revved up to go home, and I dropped in on that bar and she bought me a drink. She said there was something about my face that made her want to buy me a drink. She said I had a pretty sad face, with a comma between the 'pretty' and the 'sad.' She asked me why my eyes weren't quite blue and I told her they were hazel. She asked me why my hair was so brown and curly and my nose so big and cute, and I told her it was because they incorporated the best qualities of my Jewish and Irish genes. And we kept on talking and I told her about the shooting, and I ended up going home with her because I really didn't want to go back to my place and be alone. And the sex with her was so . . ."

I stopped speaking so quickly that I could feel my mouth still open but I couldn't close it, just sat there looking at Doc, who just kept looking back at me, a mirror reflection of frozen time. I liked this man better than anybody else I had ever known, but I never told anybody this kind of thing about me or mine. But he said she knew she had cancer when she met me, when I moved in with her, when she said she wanted to get married. Would I have married her if she had told me? I loved her. I know I loved her. It wasn't just the sex. I loved her as a person. As a woman. As a friend. I loved her. But did she love me? Or was she looking for someone to take care of her to the end? She was like me, no family. Just the two of us. Would I have married her? Would I have stayed with her? I would have. I know I would have. But why hadn't she given me the choice?

"People do crazy things when they're sick," said Doc, "crazy things that often don't make sense to those who don't have to think about exactly when they are going to die. That girl loved you, Benny. She wasn't just looking for someone to see her through to the end. I could tell that every time I was with the two of you. This past month was straight hell for you, but there are still things to do and time to do them. She's dead; it's all over. Remember the good; just remember the good."

"I better get to work," I told him. "I'm back on the payroll."

"Yeah, sure," he said. "I'm either here or at home if you need me."

I thought about that as I walked up the stairs to the file room. I thought I had needed Cathy to fill that cold hole that was always there in the pit of my stomach. But it turned out that her need was different from the one I had. And now she was gone. Her need was over. I put the palm of my hand down flat on my stomach. It was still there all right. I could feel the cold pushing in on the warm. Had it ever really gone away? I wasn't sure now. I wasn't sure about anything.

3

Moran was the kind of cop who judged everybody by whether or not they had served in the Vietnam war. No matter who he was talking to or what he was talking about, at some point he would pause for a brief moment, look them straight in the eyes, and ask: "Were you in Nam?"

This confused a lot of people, since the question almost never had anything to do with the topic under discussion. One time he even asked a nun who was a witness to an accident. The blank stare or "Huh?" never bothered him one bit. It was only when the answer was a yes or no that he reacted. If the yes was from someone Moran considered a good guy, the guy had a sympathetic ear in which to pour his troubles. If it was from a bad guy, he had an immediate enemy because to Moran everybody who had served in Vietnam was a special person, a member of a club, and if he had besmirched the escutcheon, he was in worse trouble than he might have been. One time, when we were partnered on a case, he let a lady off a big hook because it turned out she had been a nurse in Nam. It didn't bother me because she had a good reason for the terrible thing she had done, but I personally would have booked her if I'd been running the show that night. But then again, I'd never served in any war, let alone Nam.

He also resented the fact that I had been forced to shoot three people in the line of duty, killing one. And that I had been shot in the arm in the course of another investigation. Moran had never had an opportunity to shoot an American civilian in the line of duty, only "gooks" in wartime. And he had never personally been shot, either in Vietnam or in the United States. His body almost ached to be wounded heroically; you could actually feel it each time we were in a situation where guns had to be drawn.

Except for all these things, I think he liked me about as much as he liked anybody. When I told Cathy that once, she said it was true because she was sure that Moran didn't really like anybody. All in all, even though he could only think in straight lines, he was a tough, honest cop who would back you to his limit, and that was good enough for me.

"I've been working like a dog on this case," said Moran, "and the captain's been giving me nothing but a hard time. I've checked out everything. Every car that's been sold off this lot the past six months in case somebody bought a lemon and got even the hard way. I checked into those Vietnam gangs that have been putting the squeeze on Vietnamese businessmen. Christ, I even checked into tong wars. But this was one clean guy. He was a lieutenant commander in the Vietnamese navy, and the Pentagon gave him a clean bill when we sent an inquiry. He worked hard, made honest deals, good to his family. There's nothing. I don't know what the hell the captain expects you to come up with after all I've done to—"

"He just wants to get me out of his hair for a few weeks," I said.

"What?"

"I came back to work all of a sudden, and he didn't know what to do with me. So he stuck me on this. It's got nothing to do with you or the job you've done. He just wants me out of his way."

"Oh," said Moran, and I could see him relaxing, even a little upset with himself for thinking that I was somehow mixed up in something to put him down. He heaved a big sigh, and went so far as to put a hand on my shoulder. But whatever he was going to say was interrupted by one of the most beautiful women I had ever seen in my life.

She was slight except for her eyes and her breasts, which were queen-sized, complementing each other perfectly, almond to round. I thought of one of the diamonds I had encountered when I was looking for an engagement ring for Cathy, perfect from every angle, the salesman had said. It was too expensive.

There were black circles under her eyes that indicated a lack of sleep, a deep sorrow, but even these melted into the creamy cheeks with just the right shading. I could tell by the look on Moran's face that this was a good Vietnamese.

"Ah, Sergeant Moran," she said in English whose only touch of foreignness was more French than Asian, "you perhaps bring news for us?"

"I'm sorry," said Moran, "but there have been no new developments. I have been assigned to another case, and Sergeant Freedman is taking charge."

She turned slightly to look me over, and I mean look me over. This was not just an inspection by a used-car dealer's daughter, which in California can be most suspicious indeed. This was the look of someone who had survived a war by checking each and every person encountered right through to the bone marrow. She had learned her lesson the hard way.

"How do you do, Sergeant," she said formally, a hint of a bow accompanying the words. "I hope you will be able to find and punish the slayer of my husband."

Husband! The slayer of her husband. I looked more closely. Twenty-three at most. And that was giving away points. I had only seen photographs of the husband after he had been garotted, so it was impossible to tell if he had looked young for his age, but this woman couldn't be more than twenty-three. Which brought sex into the case.

"What is your age, please?" I asked.

Moran gargled something in his throat, but Mrs. Dienben was nonplussed.

"I have forty-five years," she said, "a have three daughters and two sons, in age from twenty-three years to nineteen years."

"Thank you," I said, echoing her slight bow. I had no idea how to get from there to any place else, so I pulled the little stack of index cards from my shirt pocket and jotted down her age and those of her children.

The index cards were something I had picked up from my father, who used them as a weapon as well as a memory tool. He stuck the cards and the pen in his shirt each morning in the same way he put his wallet in his back pocket and his change in his side pocket and his watch on his wrist. If I happened to goof, either up or off, during the day, out would come a card and the pen and the alleged offense would be noted down.

"Okay, boychik," he would say, "it's all here in black and white, official." And it never failed to scare the hell out of me.

But mainly he used it because he was an absent-minded artist whose thoughts were on musical rather than mental notes, and if he didn't write down that there was an extra rehearsal scheduled for Thursday or that my mother had asked him to bring home a loaf of bread, he would miss the rehearsal or we would go breadless that day.

Once I was big enough to reach the copycat stage, I would also stick paper and a pen in my pocket, even though I didn't know the difference between an A and a B, and I would go around pretending I was making notes, especially if one of my playmates did me dirty.

And by the time I could tell the difference between an A and a B, I found the notetaking a most useful habit that I continued to utilize to this day. Just as my father used to scare me, so I would pull out the cards and pen and note down things being said by prisoners or witnesses being interrogated. It was an incredible gimmick to hype the tension. And it was amazing how many times some little thing I had noted down turned out to be an important factor in solving a case or helping to convict a perpetrator.

It became a kind of crutch for me, something to do when I didn't know what else to do. So right now, if ever I needed them, I had in my possession the ages of Mrs. Dienben and all her children, part of Benny's card-index memory bank.

Moran was impatient to get on with it, and started striding toward the little office building behind the first line of shiny used cars. Mrs. Dienben looked at his back, then at me, and when she realized I was going to wait for her to precede, she started after Moran. After three steps she turned her head quickly to look at me, as if to check on where my eyes might be glued. She nodded, a wisp of a smile on her face, and then walked quickly to the office.

There I met two of the children, the older son and youngest daughter, who stood up from their little desks and remained standing, faces impassive, the whole time we were there. They also had deep circles under their eyes.

"Let me show you where the . . . ah . . . perpetration took place," said Moran, and he led the way across the lot, followed again by Mrs. Dienben and then me. He went directly across the black pavement to a line of cars in the rear against a six-foot-high wire fence with three strands of barbs a foot above that.

"Hey," said Moran, "the car is back. The lab must have finished with it."

"We were called to pick it up two days ago," said Mrs. Dienben. "I did not want to bring it back here, but our eldest son . . . my eldest son, said that it would be foolish to just . . . that my husband would want . . . that we . . ."

"It is not necessary for you to be here," I told her. "Sergeant Moran can fill me in, and then if there are any questions, I can check with you in the office."

"No, no," she said, straightening her body into a mannikin rigidity, "it is proper I accompany and assist you."

"Well," said Moran, walking around to the driver's side of the car, "this is where . . ."

He froze where he was, slightly bent over to look into the car interior, his face and hands beet red as though an invisible blow to the solar plexus had pile-driven the blood into all the extremities of his body.

I had my gun in my hand by the time I leapt the three steps separating us, but at first I could see nothing to have caused such a violent reaction. But as my eyes made the second sweep, I focused right on it almost immediately. There on the passenger side, neatly enclosed in a clear plastic bag, was a human finger, and Doc's words echoed in my brain: *neatly severed by a bolt cutter.*

Mrs. Dienben ran to the other side of the car and started banging her fists against the window, pulling futilely on the locked door handle, tears streaming down her face, screaming something in Vietnamese or English, it was impossible to tell.

Moran turned and shoved me out of the way, running as hard as he could toward the office. By the time he came back with the older son and the keys to the car, I was holding Mrs. Dienben in my arms, cradling her as softly as I could but forced to use some strength to keep her from busting her hands on the glass.

The young man opened the door and the blast of hot air that came out also had the stench of decay in it. Mrs. Dienben kept trying to reach the little packet, but I held her tightly and Moran prevented the boy from reaching in on the other side.

"Evidence," Moran was yelling. "Evidence."

"That is my brother's finger," the young man yelled. "That is my brother's finger."

"Where is your brother?" Moran yelled, even louder.

"We don't know," the boy said in a low-pitched wail that echoed his mother. "He has been gone for three days. We don't know."

4

Some police-department snitch made himself a hundred bucks about an hour after we returned to headquarters, and the reporters and TV cameras were all over the used-car lot by noon.

The captain teamed me and Moran, making me senior, which had to grab Moran by both cheeks, but at the moment he seemed relieved that he didn't have to decide which direction was forward.

As we were about to leave the office, the captain motioned for me to stay. Moran hesitated at the door a moment, then went out. It was obviously going to take a while to convince him that we were really partners in the mess and that my being chosen as king of the hill was only a formality brought on by the captain's desire to cause trouble among us lower ranks. The captain immediately spelled it out.

"Don't get to thinking that you're any better than Moran on this case," he said. "But he's already burned himself out on it, and this might light his fire again. As a matter of fact, he's a better detective than you all round. You use a lot of fancy words from God knows where, but that don't mean shit to a detective. What you do have going for you is drive. When you bounce off something, you keep going in the new direction. You don't just sit there shifting the finger that was in your mouth to your asshole and vice versa. You keep moving.

"Now, this case is going to be front-page for a while again, and we're going to get heat from all directions. If Bello's ulcer hadn't blown a hole through his stomach, there'd be a lieutenant running this show. But right now it's up to you two. With my nose just this far from your assholes. And I'd better smell something sweet by the end of the week."

I almost thanked him for his inspiring speech, but his head had already dropped down to the papers on his desk again. This was the first time he'd ever paid me even a backward compliment, and it gave me a funny feeling in my stomach. He was right about my abilities. The promotion to detective had come from taking on barehanded two punks with knives in an attempted liquor-store heist. They quit as soon as they realized I meant it. And the promotion to sergeant had come from taking out a guy on the FBI list when he tried to make get-out-of-town money in another attempted liquor-store heist. He had a gun and didn't quit even when he realized I meant it. If it weren't for liquor stores, I'd still be walking a beat. I had studied two years of criminology at a community college in Boston, and when I first became a patrolman in California, I took out some books on deduction and investigative technique from the library, but I never ran across anything that came close to the examples in the books. We stamped "Solved" on maybe four out of ten cases we handled, and that was usually because it was the brother-in-law or the estranged husband or eight witnesses fingered the guy. Moran probably was a better detective than I was, but my case record was as good as his. Because, just as the captain said, I was a bouncer, and I kept bouncing until there were no more places to bounce.

I told Moran to get together all his reports and round up all the other information on the case and leave it on my desk. I called the used-car lot and one of the daughters told me her mother was at home. I asked for the address and she gave it to me. My experience with Orientals was that they either clammed up entirely or cooperated completely. The Dienbens were obviously depending on their new nation's constabulary to help them in their hour of need.

A TV mobile van was pulling away from the house as I got there, and Mrs. Dienben opened the door for me before I could ring the bell.

"You don't have to talk to those people, you know," I told her. "Do you have a lawyer to advise you on this matter?"

"I have discussed the matter with a friend acquainted with the law," she said. "I am also willing to talk to the newspeople so that I can plead with whoever has my son. There is no other way to reach these people. I do not know who they are. I do not know what they want. Why should anyone kill my husband and then take my son? I thought we had escaped all that. I thought the nightmare was over."

Usually when I have nothing to say, I say nothing. But her anxiety was such that I felt I had to fill the void, and words came out of my mouth.

"Everything's going to be all right," I told her.

The look she gave me was a mixture of pity and disgust. So much for Oriental inscrutability.

"I know you are trying to help, Sergeant," she

said, "and I appreciate what you are doing. But I have lost my husband forever, and all I have of my youngest son is the first finger of his right hand. He is probably lost forever, too. You can know nothing of my loss, my grief. Please, just do your job as best you can. What can you know of loss, of grief?"

She broke the dam with that. For two days I had bricked over the hole, worked every minute on the case without thinking of anything else, reading the reports, the files, taking notes, anything to keep going, until it was impossible to keep my eyes open. And even then I didn't take any chances, knocking back two of the pills Doc had given me when he had cautioned me to take only one. But all those pills bought me was three hours of twitching sleep before I woke again at six and started right in again.

It was now nearly three in the afternoon, and I was so tired I could feel each joint of my body where bone connected to bone. And the lady had asked me what could I know about loss, about grief.

I didn't make any noise, but the tears started pouring out of my eyes and running down my face, a seemingly endless stream that I could feel dripping off the sides of my chin. The last time I had cried like that had been when my father died, and just before they closed the coffin on him, one of his old friends from the Boston Symphony had stuck out his hand so that the undertaker couldn't lower the lid. And then Meyer had straightened each one of my father's twisted fingers as best he could, maybe hoping that it would help him to play the violin again in heaven.

Dupuytren's contractures, the doctor had called it. I wrote it down so I had all the letters straight.

Dupuytren's contractures. It turned his ring finger and little finger into twisted claws. The tissue under your palm thickens and shrinks until your fingers twist up at the knuckles. It runs in families, the doctor said, especially with alcoholics and epileptics. My father finally had the operation, but within a year his fingers had turned back to little twigs. Remembering his frustration, his hopelessness, his reason for swallowing all those pills, I started to sob as the coffin lid finally came down and I kept crying until the last shovelful of dirt was thrown at the cemetery. Sometimes when I was out shooting at the police range, I would look at my ring and little finger twisted around the handle of the gun and I would think of my father.

Mrs. Dienben watched me for a moment and then did what I had done for her in the car lot, cradled me to her, her small body somehow surrounding me as the past four months washed out of me in receding waves. I knew I was all right again as I began to think of how it might look if Moran or another TV crew stumbled in, and as soon as she sensed this, the lady let me go.

"Will you take a cup of tea with me?" she asked.

Before I could answer, she looked at my face closely and spoke again.

"When did you last eat food, Sergeant?"

I didn't want to acknowledge the wetness on my face by taking my handkerchief out, so I just kept rubbing my eyes with my right fist as if the sockets needed polishing. She took me by the arm and led me into the kitchen, where she sat me down by the highly polished pine table.

"What have you lost, Sergeant?" she asked so softly that I wasn't sure whether the words were coming from her or out of my head.

"My wife," I heard my voice say.

She nodded, almost as if she had expected that answer.

"I have lost a husband and you have lost a wife. We are fated to help each other. I am confident that you will return my son."

She gathered my face in both her hands and touched her cool lips to my forehead. Her lips were so red that I reached up to feel how much lipstick was stuck to the skin, but there was nothing there, nothing. I moved my fingers to her lips and there was no lipstick there either, and I wanted to kiss this woman, to press my skin against her red, red skin. She did not move. God knows what she would have allowed in the sharing and shoring of our two losses. Or what I would have done.

But a ringing telephone can never be denied, and the one on the wall of the kitchen sounded a clarion for both of us. She turned and answered it, identified herself, and then told some reporter that she had nothing to add to the information she had given earlier.

She went from the phone to the refrigerator without looking at me, and busied herself carrying pots and pans and jars and bowls to the stove and the counter, chopping vegetables and slicing wafer-thin pieces of meat, oiling a huge wok and setting out plates and utensils on the table before me.

About halfway through the meal, which increased my appetite with each bite, the two daughters came in, pale reflections of their mother, and after brief introductions, they sat down and silently began to pack away huge amounts of rice interspersed with small amounts of meat and vegetables. It was as if we were a real family, one that didn't need to make useless conversation.

My appetite stopped as quickly as it began, and I suddenly realized that if I took one more bite, I would lose everything. When I stopped eating, everybody stopped eating, and after a few moments, Mrs. Dienben and the girls stood up and started clearing everything away.

"You have questions you wish to ask me, Sergeant?" said Mrs. Dienben.

"Please."

"We will go in the living room while my daughters finish here," she said, and led me through the door to a room furnished in Ethan Allen pine. How far away can you get from Vietnam?

"Now," she said when we had settled down on the sofa, "what is it you wish to know?"

"Where were you educated, madam?" I asked.

I was the only one surprised by my saying "madam"; she sort of took it for granted. She did cock her head to one side a bit as if trying to decide what the hell that question had to do with the price of fish. Maybe in the back of my mind I was trying to find some angle, some new direction that Moran hadn't investigated. Maybe I just wanted to know more about her.

"I was educated in France," she said, "which is where I also learned English. From an American lady, Mrs. Travers. I have been told that I speak English like a French person from South Dakota. Which is where Mrs. Travers came from originally. You also speak English somewhat differently."

"I was born in Boston," I told her. "My father was a violinist with the Boston Symphony until"— even now it was hard to think of it—"until he had to retire."

"And your mother?"

"My mother was a barmaid. An Irish barmaid. A

classic Irish barmaid. She died when I was eleven. She died of the drink. One day my father's fingers started turning and twisting in all directions. They tried all kinds of medicines and wonder drugs and even surgery, but they kept twisting and turning until he couldn't play the violin anymore. He had to retire from the orchestra on a disability pension. But he couldn't stand not playing the violin anymore. And he kept trying. Which made him very unhappy. So he started drinking instead of playing. He was a pretty good drinker to begin with, which is how he met my mother, but he became the Kreisler of drinkers, the Yehudi Menuhin, the Paganini. And my mother drank to keep him company. But she didn't have the liver for it, and she died. When I was eleven. My father's liver was much stronger and he didn't die until I was twenty-two. But even then he had to do it by swallowing a handful of pills along with a bottle of vodka. His liver wouldn't quit. So he did."

Well, I thought to myself, this interrogation is going pretty good. If I ask her just one more question, she'll know my whole life story.

"When, Sergeant, when did your wife die?"

"Monday."

"Monday!"

"Monday. And you want to know why I am back at work so quickly. Because I have nowhere else to go. Work is a place to go. And my work is homicide. Which is why I am sitting here pouring out my guts to you, Mrs. Dienben. I should be doing something to help you, that's what I'm paid for, and all I'm doing is wallowing in my own self-pity. I think maybe the doctor was right. I shouldn't have made believe I could come back to work so soon. There are too many things I have to figure out in my own life before I can help anybody else figure out theirs."

She reached out her hand and touched me on the arm.

"No, Sergeant," she said, "I feel that fate has had a hand in this. I have never been a religious person, but I do feel that there are times when people or events are brought together for some greater reason. I cannot imagine why any higher being would want my husband murdered so horribly and my son taken away from me. How did your wife die?"

"Cancer."

"Ah. I cannot imagine why any higher being would inflict what has happened on me, and I am sure you are just as puzzled as to why this has happened to you."

Her eyes filled with tears and she was unable to speak. I started to reach my hand out to hers, but caught myself in time. Was I there to hold a double wake or was I there to find out who murdered her husband and kidnapped her son? I stood up.

"Mrs. Dienben," I said, "I feel I am not accomplishing what I should here, and I must go. Tomorrow, after I have gone over every aspect of the case, I will return and question you properly. I want to thank you for your sympathy, for your delicious dinner, and your cooperation. Good night."

I turned and went out to the hall before she could rise from the couch, and went straight out the front door, closing it with a bigger bang than I intended.

As I got in the car, I realized that I felt better, that my head had cleared. It could have been the food I had eaten. It could have been because I was with somebody whose troubles were even worse than mine. She had a son out there somewhere minus a finger and maybe even minus his life. I couldn't do anything about her husband, and she couldn't do anything about my Cathy. But I could damn well do something about her son, and I was damn well going to.

5

Moran had left all the papers and photographs on my desk, and I worked until seven P.M. going over everything, including the stuff I had already sifted through twice. Moran and his team had been thorough, there was no doubt about that, and there was nothing new I could put my finger on, no stone I could see that hadn't already been turned over and scraped.

The one thing that did bother me was that there had been no tips from the street, no calls from the regular pieces of flotsam who were looking to pick up twenty bucks for something they had heard in a bar. It was rare that the street was so quiet with a killing like this. There was some tiny twist that I was missing, something that had to be a little out of place. I piled everything neatly and started again right from the beginning.

I had only reached the second page of the report when Molly Lincoln, who had twice worked decoy with me in hotel stakeouts, pulled a chair up beside me and sat down. She was a good cop; you didn't ever have to worry about your back when she was your partner.

"Hey, Benny," she said, putting her hand around my arm, "how you doing?"

"I'm working on it," I told her.

"Look," she said, "tomorrow's my day off. Why don't I go to your apartment and pack up clothes and things? You wouldn't even have to be there. You just tell me what you want done with them."

I could feel my eyeballs getting wet again, and I wondered what would happen in the squad room if I started dripping all over the place. Would Molly pull me to her bosom the way Mrs. Dienben had? Or would the captain come out and hug me till I was all better? That thought dried me right up, and I was even able to speak without getting clogged in the throat.

"Molly," I said, "that's really considerate of you, and I appreciate the offer, but I think right now I'd like to leave everything where it is. I don't want any magic wands to wave and make everything disappear like it had never been there in the first place. I feel I'd like to do it a little bit at a time."

She thought about that for a few seconds, her eyes studying my face like she was going to have to describe it in court.

"My mother did that with my father's stuff," she said softly, "and it was like pressing a hot iron to her belly every day. But if that's what you want right now, I'm not going to argue. If and when you change your mind, the offer holds."

She held her stare on my face until our eyes met, and then she smiled.

"Look," she said, "I'm meeting my husband for some supper at Angelo's. Would you like to come along and eat with us? I think I can even get Mr. Cheapo to pick up the tab."

I tried to crack my lips in a smile that would match hers, but the muscles wouldn't work.

"Thanks," I told her, "but I ate just a little while ago. I have these reports to go through and—"

_____

"Benny," she said, "I was watching you before I came over. You're not seeing anything. You're just turning pages. Why don't you go home and get some sleep, and go at it real hard tomorrow?"

It was as if her words were like heavy weights on my head. I was suddenly so tired that I could barely keep from trembling as I sat there. I nodded and she gave my arm a squeeze and moved back to her own desk.

I left the car in the police lot and took a taxi home. We lived on the top floor of an old brownstone that someone had copied from New York seventy-five years before, and by the time I had climbed the three flights of steps to my door, I was puffing for breath. All those weeks of sitting and watching and waiting had sucked the strength from my body. But the small soft hand that used to slide over my flat belly, the fingertips probing out each strand of muscle, was no longer there. Nothing was there.

My head was down as I tried to separate the door key from the six others on the ring, and I didn't see the two men until I raised my eyes in conjunction with my hand to insert the key in the lock.

The older one looked to be in his mid-fifties, and from his silver-white hair to his cordovan shoes he spelled both money and power. The alligator briefcase was the crowning touch. As you looked at it, you could almost picture the rednecks in the boat in the Southern swamp, the rifle at the shoulder ready to shoot the raw material for this particular briefcase. Nothing went into that receptacle that didn't have to do with making or breaking somebody or some thing.

The younger guy, probably in his late thirties, was about four steps down the ladder from the other one, but you had the feeling his hands were reaching for the next rung or maybe even the one above it. His suit was a bit more rakishly cut, and might even have been off an expensive rack, but you could tell he never boogalooed on Saturday night. His briefcase was plain old real leather.

"Sergeant Freedman?" asked the older one.

I nodded, my hand with the key still extended toward the door.

"I am Dwayne Hamilton and this is Arnold Wenker. We have some business with you."

"Of what nature?"

"I am a lawyer and he is a banker, and it has to do with your wife's estate. One of your neighbors was good enough to let us in the ground-floor door so that we might wait for you up here. If we may intrude upon you, we will explain our purpose as quickly as possible and then leave you to your privacy."

Dwayne Hamilton. Lawyer. Hamilton, Slater, and Silverman. Big law firm. The biggest. Dwayne Hamilton. Friend of the mayor. Friend of the governor. Friend of the president. Friend of whoever was mayor, governor, or president at any particular time. Friend of everybody who was anybody. What the hell would he have to do with my wife's estate? Our joint checking account came to something like thirty-four hundred dollars. The funeral director had said that the whole thing would cost about two thousand, give or take a hundred. Dwayne Hamilton probably tipped more than our estate was worth wringing wet.

I unlocked the door, stepped inside to turn on the light, and then motioned them in. They stood in the entryway, holding their briefcases just below present arms, and waited for the next move. I went ahead putting on lights and finally had them seated in the living room. Cathy would have been upset about having company see the apartment in this sloppy condition. When I came home from work, the place always looked like the chambermaid had just left. Even when she was so sick she could barely hold her head up, she somehow kept all the rooms looking neat and tidy. It was almost like she might have to go away all of a sudden, and she didn't want anybody to know she had been there.

I had nothing to say to them so I waited. Hamilton, as soon as he realized the situation, got right to it.

"Your wife, Catherine, left quite a sizable estate, Sergeant Freedman," he said.

"There's enough to cover the funeral," I told him.

"Oh, there's quite a bit more than that," he said. "Much more than that. I take it that you are unaware of exactly how much."

"Mrs. Freedman informed us that her husband knew nothing of her means," the younger guy said, "and the situation was to remain the same until her death."

For the first time in I didn't know how long, I felt anger rise in my body and could feel the red pumping into my face. Who was this glossy son of a bitch who said he knew something about my wife that I didn't know? What the hell was going down?

"I know who you are," I told Hamilton, "but who is this guy?"

"Mr. Wenker is with the Bay City Bank of Upsala, New York," said Hamilton, "a county seat close to the Canadian border. The Bay City Bank is the repository of your wife's trust fund, which has been left entirely to you. The bank has asked me to represent them, and you also, if you wish, in completing the terms of the will and following your desires in the use or uses of the estate."

"What's this all about?" I said. "Let's skip the lawyer talk and the banker talk, and spell it out in one sentence."

"You've inherited a great deal of money," said Hamilton. "Something over six million dollars. That's two sentences, I know, but it's difficult to do six million in one."

Maybe Dwayne Hamilton made small jokes, but he didn't make big jokes, and there had to be a big joke in there somewhere.

"There is no way that my wife could have had an estate of six million dollars," I said. "She didn't look it; she didn't act it; she didn't have it. There's a mistake here somewhere. I don't know what it is, but there's got to be a mistake. Another lady of the same name. Another Benny Freedman. Six million sounds great. But it can have nothing to do with me."

Hamilton looked at the younger guy.

"There's no mistake," the banker said. "I was personally in charge of your wife's account, and was in constant touch with her until a month before her death. And you are the Benjamin Freedman to whom the money has been left. The Bay City Bank doesn't make mistakes in matters like this. Everything has been checked and double-checked."

"We never had a phone bill that had one call to whatever city you're from in New York," I told him. "We never had any calls to the East."

"Your wife had a phone credit card that was billed directly to the bank, and believe me, Sergeant Freedman, all the calls are there. She phoned us every week while she was able, and when she became too ill to make the calls or because you were at her side constantly, we had Mr. Hamilton's office monitor the situation."

"Everything has been discreet," said Hamilton. "No one else knows anything about any of this."

"Where did this money come from?" I asked.

"We are not at liberty to discuss the history of the trust," said the banker. "The money is now yours to do with as you wish, but that is as far as it goes."

"If I said that I wanted it all, in cash, tomorrow, you would just hand it over?"

"No," said the banker, "it wouldn't be that simple. There are numerous investments. A great deal could be turned over tomorrow, but the bulk would take some time, anywhere from ninety days to two years."

"My wife said she had no family," I told them. "She said her mother had died of cancer"—that word stopped me for a few seconds when for the first time I realized what heredity had done to my Cathy—"and that her father had been killed in an accident. She didn't say what kind of accident; I just assumed it was a car accident. She said she came from the East two years ago and that she had worked as a secretary, except she wasn't working anywhere when I met her. She said she'd bought this apartment with the money from her father's insurance, figuring it was a good investment at the time. Since my place was only a sublease, I moved in with her. But even the upkeep was more than we could reasonably afford, and I kept telling her we were going to have to sell it for something smaller. When I told her that, she never said a word about being able to pay for it if she wanted. She just nodded like that was the way it was going to be. We lived on my salary. Except for this place, she never kicked in a dime for anything. It doesn't make sense. Why would she sit on six million bucks like that? I'm a cop. A detective! And I didn't have a clue. Not a clue. The whole thing stinks."

"Look," said the banker, "the original trust was set up with five million dollars and it has accrued something over a million more because your wife took almost nothing out of it. Whenever I talked to her on the phone, I would always end by asking if we could send some money, and she'd always say no. 'We're doing fine,' she'd say. Our job was to handle her trust exactly as she wanted it. If she wanted to let the funds build up, that was her business. And now it's your business. That's why we're here. To find out what you want to do with it. Do you want lump sums, weekly payments? Do you want us to continue being administrator or do you want to change? We'd like to keep the account, and you must admit we've done awfully well with it, but it's your prerogative. Do you want to take charge of the investments or continue letting our trust department handle it? We're here to serve."

"What about taxes and all that crap?"

"That's all being taken care of."

"Who knows about this? Are the newspapers and television going to be full of stories about the homicide cop who inherited six million dollars?"

"The bank has great discretion in this matter," said Hamilton. "Everything has been filed in that little upstate city in New York, and all the public officials there are most cooperative. Unless you yourself tell or there is some factor which has been overlooked, which I strongly doubt, no one else need know about it."

"Look," I said, "I'm in no shape to take any of this in. It's just not real. Give me a few more days to work my way through Cathy's . . . Cathy's . . ."

"Of course," said Hamilton, getting to his feet.

"Your loss is still uppermost in your mind, and I must apologize again for the intrusion. But Mr. Wenker had his official function to perform according to your wife's wishes. Why don't we leave things as they are right now, and when you are ready, call me at my office. This card has my private number on it, and my secretary will put you right through."

"I must return to Upsala first thing in the morning," said Wenker, "but I can fly out whenever needed. I took the liberty of bringing along a check for fifty thousand dollars to cover any untoward expenses you might have."

He held the slip of paper out toward me.

"I'm all right for now," I told him.

"Why don't you just deposit it," he said, "and then in case—"

"Look," I told him, "do you know what could happen if a homicide cop suddenly deposited fifty thousand dollars in a bank out of nowhere?"

Hamilton grinned and somehow I grinned back at him. He knew the score. Wenker returned the check to a pocket inside his briefcase. They expressed sorrow for the first time over the loss of my wife, we shook hands, and they left. Just before he went out the door, Hamilton paused to look back at me for a moment. He was a guy who was used to dealing in millions, and it was no big deal to him for another guy to join the club. Hell, all kinds of people were winning lotteries all over the country, and it was no longer considered crazy for a guy hitting .260 to play for two million bucks a year. But this was somewhat different with me having no idea I was married to a lady who sat on six million bucks without giving me the slightest hint. He was probably wondering what kind of marriage it was.

And in the back of my mind, just the slightest tickle, something was wondering about that too.

I don't know how long I stared at the door before I went to our bedroom and started pulling things out of Cathy's closet. I did the standard police search, feeling through the clothes and then the top shelf. Nothing. There was a pile of shoe boxes on the left-hand side of the floor, and inside one of them was a clutch purse which had a phone credit card, a MasterCard, and an American Express card, all made out to Catherine Freedman, but there was no address on any of the plastic. There was, however, one MasterCard receipt in the purse for the videocassette recorder she had given me for Christmas, and the clerk had made her write her address and phone number on the bottom. It said Bay City Bank, Upsala, NY, and the phone number had an area code I didn't recognize. A very solid piece of evidence, Mr. District Attorney.

My rummaging had knocked one of her dresses off the hanger, and I picked it up from the floor and took it with me to the bed, where I sat holding it to my face, her sweet aroma everywhere around and inside me.

You think you get to know a person when you live with them for a period of time. Not just how they smell—everything. Cathy and I had fit together right from that very first night we met; something had melted inside of me and fused into her. Whoever had dreamed up the words "in sickness and in health" in the marriage vows knew what he was talking about, because that's the other thing that breaks down the barriers. When you stand with a wrung-out washcloth alongside somebody throwing up so that you can wipe their lips clean or cool their forehead, or listen to somebody in the throes of diarrhea, or hold somebody close whose body is burning up with fever, you have to believe that there are no secrets left, that you know everything there is to know. And when you make love the way we had made love, you feel the other person is you. Not just part of you, but you yourself.

I knew my Cathy, I still didn't doubt that. I knew the person that I loved and I knew that she loved me. But she had a big secret from me in her body, and now another secret in her mind. She didn't tell me about the cancer, and she didn't tell me about any six million dollars. Those were two big secrets —death and money.

I was so grateful that I had found her, that she was there, that I didn't really care where she had come from, only where we were going. I always felt that I had never had a family even when my mother and father were still alive, and that I had no family after that, even though there were aunts and uncles and cousins somewhere in Ireland. We had joked a couple of times about going to Ireland and surprising them, and I had asked Cathy if she perhaps also had some Irish blood in her, but all she did was an imitation of a jig before knocking me over backward on the couch and kissing my face a hundred times. She never gave me an answer about what kind of blood she had in her.

Cathy and I were a team, a pair, a couple, but we weren't a family. A family involves kids, and the thought of children had only passed fleetingly through my mind. I was wondering what had passed through her mind. Had she ever thought of having children? Mostly we kept to ourselves, but a couple of times we had been invited to a fellow cop's house for dinner, and she had been pleasant to the children, but she'd made no big deal about them. She had never mentioned that she wanted children someday. I suppose when a woman knows she has incurable cancer, the last thing she thinks about is having a baby. She's concentrating on endings, not beginnings.

I wrapped the dress around my fist and pounded the mattress, trying to knock some sense out of something. Where had she come from to begin with? Once she had mentioned something about living in New Jersey, but she said it like it was the beginning of a joke she never got around to telling. Once she had quoted something that a teacher had said in college, but there was no follow-up to that and we had gone on to something else.

I sat there running memories through my head like dirt through a sieve, shaking the stones on the top of the wire, running my fingers through the fine sand on the ground, but nothing new came out. There had been no stories of brothers or sisters or cousins or aunts. And since I had no stories of my own, it didn't seem peculiar that she had none either.

Where would she have gotten five million dollars that had grown into six? My father had always said that poor people stayed poor because they could only earn as much as they could do with their hands, while rich people became rich from the money they made from other people's hands. He was bitter because his living came from what his hands could do to a violin, and when his hands went, so did his living. I only earned what I could with my hands, or maybe it was more from my feet. But six million dollars! It took a lot of hands to gather together six million dollars. What kind of money was it? And why didn't she want to use it except for an apartment and presents for me?

I unwrapped the dress from my fist and tried to smooth it out on the bed with the flat of my hand, but the material had wrinkled and wouldn't return to its former condition. That was happening to Cathy at that very moment inside that box down in the dirt.

I took my hand off the dress and put my fingers under my eyes to check, but it was all dry there. The crying was over. But I doubt that at that moment there was an unhappier millionaire anywhere in the world. Anywhere.

6

The captain pulled Moran off my detail the very next day to handle a murder in a gay bar that had occurred when four stallions found out they were not exclusively shoeing the same mare. In the old days, this would not have caused anything but terribly hurt feelings, but since the AIDS trauma, fidelity had become important to some of these guys. Assigning Moran was typical of the captain. Moran became psychotic when he had to deal with gays, even if they'd served in Vietnam. On one occasion it reached the point where Molly Lincoln had joked that maybe Moran had a problem he didn't know about. Nobody, including me, even considered the possibility for a second, but nobody laughed either. Moran was one of those guys who couldn't handle aberrations, which was probably why he became a cop in the first place, but it was mean of the captain to put him on this one. It would have been better to assign me, and the whole thing probably could have been wrapped up in a couple of days. But the way Moran was, he could be gone for the duration.

I went back and interrogated Mrs. Dienben and the children and the three salesmen on the lot, only one of whom was a native American, but couldn't come up with anything new. Mrs. Dienben kept hoping for a ransom note for her son, but there was nothing, nothing at all, and even the newspapers stopped writing those little stories that said the police had as yet made no progress. The murder and kidnapping were still too new for the scandal papers and magazines to write their bizarre interpretations of what had "really" happened, and by the end of the week there was just me slogging around trying to stir up mud in a dry streambed.

One day had become pretty much like another, but my eye happened to catch the calendar on my desk and this particular one turned out to be a Friday. Perkins, who handled the late shift, was meticulous about tearing the pages off the calendar and sharpening whatever pencils were in the drawer and even wiping down the top once in a while with damp paper towels. He wasn't much of a detective because his gun had more brains than he did, but he sure knew how to janitor a desk.

My watch, which kept the correct time because of the battery inside it, told me it was nine o'clock. I didn't think I had eaten any supper so I went downstairs to see if maybe Doc was working late, and sure enough he was hunched over the phone, the mouthpiece plastered against his lips.

"Don't worry about it," he muttered into the phone, "we'll work something out. Don't worry about it."

I started to back out the door but he motioned me in and pointed to a chair. He turned his back to me after I sat down, and lowered his voice, but I could still hear him well enough. There isn't that much noise in the morgue after the official workday has ended.

"We'll get it," he said. "Don't worry about it. We'll work something out. I've got somebody here. I'll be home in a little while. Don't worry about it."

After he hung up, he took a moment to himself before he turned around, but by the time he did, he had that soft smile on his face.

"How's it going?" he asked.

"With who?"

"With who? With you, of course. That's who."

"I'm doing all right. How are you doing?"

"Me! I'm doing fine."

"I don't think you are. I may not be enough of a detective to have made any progress on the case I'm on, but I'm enough of a detective to know that you are not doing fine. What's wrong?"

His whole body sagged, and he sank down into the chair behind him the way my father used to when his fingers went bad. The Doc, who had seen me through the worst four months of my life, the rock, was being broken into rubble right before my eyes. But he still wasn't going to talk.

"Doc," I said, "you saved my life. You owe me. What's wrong?"

He shrugged his big shoulders, the kind of shrug a guy makes just before he tells you that, yeah, that was his knife and there had been an argument.

"You know those nuclear plants up north," he said, "the ones that went bust before they were even finished?"

I nodded.

"We put everything we had into those bonds," he said. "Everything. And two weeks after that I co-signed a note for our son for eighteen thousand dollars so he could add it to his own holdings and buy into the business he always wanted. And the business went bust and they're calling the note. This has not been a good year for the men in my family."

And he gave me that little grin of his. Only it was a very tired grin this time around. Dead tired.

I sat there staring at him, not knowing what to say. Eighteen thousand dollars. Jesus. Doc must have made twice to maybe even three times what I did, and would be getting a pretty good pension when he retired. But he had tapped himself out going for a luxury pension and a wad to leave his son. Even Cathy and I . . . Cathy. Cathy and I.

I dug my wallet out of my pocket and searched through the mess until I found Hamilton's card with his secretary's name on it. There it was. Desmond Tivy. And the number. I pulled the phone toward me and dialed. It rang three times before there was a click and a metallic voice came on.

"This is Desmond Tivy," said the voice. "If you are calling on Friday, I will be at 555-7311 until eleven P.M. and then at 555-6234 for the rest of the night. On Saturday, I will be . . ."

He told where he would be all day Saturday and all day Sunday until he returned to his office on Monday at eight A.M. It was obviously Desmond Tivy's job to be available at all times to whoever was given a card by Dwayne Hamilton.

I dialed the first number and the phone was answered by a woman. There was the noise of revelry behind her.

"I would like to speak to Desmond Tivy," I told her.

She didn't ask who I was or what I wanted. In a minute a very careful man's voice identified himself as Desmond Tivy.

"This is Ben Freedman," I told him.

"Yes, Mr. Freedman," he said, "what can I do for you?"

It took me a few seconds to get it out, to actually say it. I kept thinking of things the guy might come back with when I told him what I wanted.

"I need eighteen thousand dollars," I finally managed.

"Tonight?" he asked.

"Hold on a minute," I said.

"Doc." He wasn't paying attention, lost in whatever was going through his mind.

"Doc," I said, quite a bit louder.

"What? What, Benny?"

"Do you need this money tonight?"

"What?"

"The eighteen thousand dollars. Do you need it tonight or would Monday be okay?"

"What do you mean?"

"Can you wait till Monday for the money? Will Monday be too late?"

"The due date isn't for a week. Benny, what are you talking about?"

I shushed him with the hand I had been holding over the mouthpiece.

"Mr. Tivy," I said, "I don't need that money until Monday."

"Do you want it in cash or a check?"

"A check, please. Made out to Dr. Everett Wallace. I don't want my name anywhere on it. I want it made out to Dr. Wallace from a bank or whatever the hell you do."

"I understand what you are saying. Will you or he pick it up?"

"I would like it delivered to my house Monday night at seven."

"It will be there. Anything else?"

"No, thank you. And, Mr. Tivy . . ."

"Yes."

"I'm sorry I bothered you out of the office. I hope I didn't disturb your party."

"No problem, Mr. Freedman. This is my job.

Feel free to call me at any time. Any time. Good night, sir."

I held the receiver in my hand and stared at nowhere for a few seconds. When I hung up, Doc was staring at me, his mouth a little open."

"I'll bring the check to you Tuesday morning, Doc," I told him.

"Benny, you can't do this," he said. "It's eighteen thousand dollars, man. Where are you getting that kind of money? And I don't know when the hell I could pay you back in the first place."

"Cathy had an insurance policy, Doc. You know she would want you to have the money after all you did for her. For us. There's no strain. You pay it back when you can. And if you can't, there's no strain either. I've got all I need."

"No," he said. "No way. I won't take it."

"Yes, you will," I told him. "If you don't, I won't ever be able to explain to Cathy next time I meet her. Never. There's no two ways about it. I'll have it here for you Tuesday morning."

I punched him lightly on the shoulder and left before he could say anything more. We both knew he was going to take it. He didn't have any other way.

I walked down to the diner at the end of the street, nodded at the cops sitting on the stools, and took a booth in the corner by myself. As I was chewing on the cheeseburger and dipping the french fries into the catsup before popping them into my mouth, I was wondering whether somebody was going to show up Monday night with a check for eighteen thousand dollars. The guy on the phone hadn't blinked a syllable when I popped the question to him. Do you want it tonight? he had asked. Suppose I had said yes. And in cash. I had a feeling he still wouldn't have blinked, and I would have had eighteen thousand dollars to tuck under my pillow. Jesus. But what was eighteen thousand compared to six million? Did I really have six million bucks at my disposal? Monday night would tell. On Sunday I would go over the list of cars that the Dienbens had sold the six months before the murder. And on Monday I would question everybody again on what had happened the day of the murder.

But it was Monday night I was really thinking about when I planned out how to fill in the time. Monday night at seven. I stuck one of the french fries, covered with catsup, into my nose rather than my mouth. Even though the place was full of cops and detectives, nobody noticed.

7

By 7:01 I was nervous and by 7:15 I was cursing out loud, sitting in the living room with my eyes on the wall speaker that held the door buzzer. By 7:30 all the fight was out of me and I was trying to figure out what I was going to tell Doc, how I was going to explain that there wasn't any eighteen thousand dollars and I'd been had as bad as he was. Except that I could get along without the money and Doc couldn't.

What puzzled me was what Hamilton's game had been. Who was the guy who was supposed to be a banker, and why had the secretary with the phony English accent gone through the drill the way he had? Did I want it in cash or by check? They had me fooled all right. But why? Why? Why make a poor slob of a detective sergeant think he has come into six million bucks? Dwayne Hamilton didn't have to play little games with people's lives. Maybe I should call somebody at the phone company, get his private home number, and ask him the question directly. And maybe I should just let it lay where Jesus had flang it.

The buzzer rang and I was across the room before the sound waves reached the bathroom. I punched in the button and said "Yes," probably quite a bit louder than I intended.

"Mr. Benjamin Freedman?"

"Yes." The control was better.

"I have an envelope for you from Mr. Desmond Tivy."

"I'll be right down," I told him, and was as quick as my word.

The voice turned out to be a gray-haired man in a dark raincoat, holding his gray felt hat in his hand as the door opened.

"Mr. Freedman?"

"Yes."

"May I see some identification, please?"

I showed him my police card with my picture on it. He nodded as he glanced from my face to the picture, and produced a small form from his inside pocket.

"Would you sign there, please, where the X is."

I signed and received a sealed white envelope from another inside pocket. It had my name typed on the outside. This wasn't the kind of guy you offered a tip, so we both nodded each other good-bye and I returned upstairs.

Inside the envelope was a Wells Fargo cashier's check made out to Doc for eighteen thousand dollars. I couldn't wait until the next day, so I called him straight off and told him.

"Benny," he said, "I've been thinking it over, and I just can't take the money. I'll work it out some other way, but I just can't—"

"Doc," I said, "I'll see you in the morning, and I don't want to hear another word. You're beginning to piss me off."

We both laughed and when I hung up, I kept on laughing. I felt good. My Cathy was dead but she was doing good work from wherever the hell she was. And she'd left me six million bucks. The buzzer rang again.

I must have stared at it two or three minutes. I'm not even sure I breathed. Was the guy down there to get back the check? Was this phase two of some game in which nobody had told me the rules? The buzzer rang again, and I walked over, pushed the button, and said, "Yes?"

"Sergeant Benny?" It was a girl's voice.

"Who's this?"

"Darlene."

"Who?"

"Darlene. You remember me!"

There wasn't any point in debating whether or not I remembered her, so I told her to wait and walked down the stairs to the outside door again. She looked quite young and quite cute with her blond hair tied back and a dark skirt and white blouse visible through her unbuttoned light raincoat.

"Hi, Sergeant Benny," she said, and walked right past me into the hall. "You're on the top floor," she said, almost like she was explaining it to me, and started right up the stairs with me behind her. She went through my open door and stood waiting for me in the foyer. As I turned to close the door, she took off again, and I didn't catch up with her until the middle of the living room.

"This is a very nice place," she said very seriously. "Your wife had very good taste. You must miss her terribly. When I read about her dying, I wanted to come see you right away, but I didn't want to cause any embarrassment, what with what I do and with all I owe you, so I waited till now. But here I am finally and I want to tell you how sorry I am for your loss."

She walked over, put her arms around my neck, and kissed me full on the lips. It was so strange to have a soft, warm body hugging me close again

and to smell the perfume, to have my nose clogged
with the sweet aroma that lets you know that
whatever is this close is willing to do whatever the
hell you want, that I stood there for a long moment
and let my whole body go loose. But in the second
moment I noticed that the aroma was too sweet,
too strong compared to what I had been accustomed to, and I pushed out my arms and held the
girl a foot away from me.

"Who are you?" I asked.

"I told you," she said. "Darlene."

"Where do I know you from?"

"You saved my life. I'm here today only because
of you. You saved my life."

"Where? How?"

She looked at me as if I were loony. How could I
not remember something that was obviously so
important?

"The night that Raoul was going to put out my
lights. You came up behind him and gave him one
in the kidney that made him piss red for four
months. And when he went for his knife, you
kneed him in the balls and then stepped on his
face. You stepped on his face while you talked to
him. You told him who you were and how if you
ever heard that I had even one hair out of place,
even one little hair, you were going to figure that
Raoul had done it and you were going to come
back and stuff his eyeballs up his nose. Jesus!
Everybody on the fucking street knows that story. I
hustle wherever the hell I want to in this town. You
made me a princess."

I vaguely remembered what she said had happened, but it had to have been three years ago, and
Darlene looked more like a teacher's aide at a
convent school than a hooker.

"Darlene," I said, "you look . . . you look . . ."

"Oh," she said, "you didn't think I was going to come to your house in my work clothes, did you? I went out Saturday and bought this outfit. Neat, huh? I'm going to wear it one night and see who goes for this kind of look."

"Well," I said, "it was very nice of you to think of me and I certainly appreciate your coming over. Thank you very much."

She walked over and sat down on the big couch, her legs carefully placed together, her hands folded in her lap. This was obviously a much more formal call than I had figured. I had never worked vice but you get to know a lot of the street girls during investigations. Most of them were dogs when you got close up, but there were some like Darlene, attractive as hell and making more tax-free money than a good many of the local tycoons. It was surprising that she had not gone back to her pimp or taken on another one when I broke her chains that fateful night, but I felt good that I had given a hand up to an independent businesswoman. Or person. As a matter of fact, she seemed like one hell of a person.

"May I take your coat?" I asked. "Get you a drink?"

"Some white wine," she said, rising for the moment as her coat was removed.

When we were settled in, her with the wineglass held carefully by the stem and me with Scotch on the rocks, my first drink in maybe two months, she leaned back against the cushions and smiled.

"It was very nice of you to come over," I said, "and I appreciate it immensely, but you really owe me nothing. I was just doing my job, ma'am, as somebody used to say on television, and that's the end of it."

"Not with me it isn't," she said, almost heatedly.

"I have never forgotten and never will, and I came to do something for you."

"What's that?"

"I'm here to take care of you."

I had sudden visions of her moving in like a maiden aunt and cooking and cleaning and bringing me chicken soup when I had the flu.

I laughed and was instantly sorry because the hurt on her face was of major proportions.

"I'm sorry," I said. "I really appreciate the kindness of your offer, but I've already got a cleaning woman and I eat out all the time and there's a laundry and cleaning place right down the street and—"

"I'm not talking about that," she said vehemently. "I'm talking about taking care of you. You!"

"Me?"

"Yes, you. Your wife's been gone almost three weeks now, and you're a man in the prime of life. I know your kind. You don't fool around. And you've got to be hurting. Right down here you've got to be hurting." And she stuck the hand that wasn't holding her wineglass deep into the crotch of her dress.

Jesus. You're thirty-three years old and you've been a cop for eleven years, on homicide for four. You've seen it all and you've done it all. There's nothing can surprise you anymore. And I sat there speechless and stared at that girl and couldn't think of one thing to say.

"I'm clean," she said. "No herpes, no nothing. And nor having to go through no bullshit with no broad who makes you buy her dinner three times or wants to get married or have a real relationship or any of that crap. I just haul your ashes whenever you need it and go home. End of story."

You know, generosity is a complex thing. Tomorrow I was going to give Doc a check for eighteen thousand dollars and he was going to think I was the nicest, most generous person alive. But what the hell was that eighteen thousand dollars to me? It wasn't going to change my life-style one bit. If I'd had to go hungry for a year or go without a coat in the cold weather or lose the use of my right hand in order to give him the money, then I would be a hell of a guy. But what was eighteen thousand out of my six million? *Bopkes.* That's Jewish for "dried snot," according to my father. *Bopkes.*

And it was the same with Darlene. What she had just offered to give me was from the six-million wad she banked between her legs. It wasn't the same as if she was a virgin whose conscience would be killing her and whose reputation would be smeared by both God and man if she took me on for the dirty deed. *Bopkes* again.

Yet I don't know when I've been so touched by a fellow human being's attempt to reach out and do something positive and unselfish for somebody else. I almost stood up and went over to take her face between my hands and tell her how much her offer meant to me. But it wouldn't have stopped there and I knew it. Because her opening kiss and her subsequent offer had stirred something in me and I was ashamed that it had with Cathy new in her grave. I knew that time would bring me around to the world again, but it wasn't time yet. Not yet.

The silence had been long enough for Darlene to sense that things hadn't gone right for her proposal, and she looked down into her wineglass, through the glass and the floor and right down into the ground below.

"Darlene . . ." I said.

"Hey," she said, still looking down, "it was just . . . I thought . . ."

"No," I said, "no, please, listen to me. What you've just offered is a wonderful, generous thing, and you have no idea how much I appreciate it, how much it means to me. But it's still too soon for me to even think about it. I don't want to think about it yet. All her clothes are still in the closet, her things are in the rooms. She's still here for me. My wife is still here for me. And if we did it, if I accepted your offer, I would feel worse, not better. And what you want is to make me feel better. That's why you made the offer. So you can understand why it isn't right at this time. Can't you?"

She lifted her head up and I could see tears glistening in her eyes, welling up on the black mascara, and once again I had to sit tight or be lost. Only three weeks and I had to consciously sit tight. I was getting insights into my character that I didn't need at this time.

"I understand," she said. "But we wouldn't even have to screw, you know. I could give you a . . ."

A leopard's spots. The pretty face with the hair pulled back, the white blouse and the skirt, the legs primly together, they almost had me believing that Mary Poppins had come to call. I smiled at her.

"Why don't I make us a cup of coffee," I said, "and then you can get back home. I still have some work to do tonight."

When I returned from the kitchen with the tray of coffee things, I found Darlene looking at the Dienben files on my desk, the ones I had brought home to go over for the umpteenth time.

"Hey," said Darlene, "you're working on that gook case."

I closed up the folder and steered her back to the couch, where I handed her the cup of coffee.

"You know," she said, after taking a first careful sip, "I had a funny one right after that happened. The clerk called me from the Drake and said he had a john who wanted a young blond. The guy was somewhere between forty and fifty, hard to tell. Big guy with white hair. But it wasn't the kind of white hair you think about as old. More like distinguished, you know."

She took another sip of her coffee, thinking about what had happened, not sure why it had stuck in her mind like that.

"When I walked in the room," she continued, "the first thing I noticed was the little black bag on the bureau. You know, you're never sure in this business. I've been lucky but you never know what the next time is going to be. And when I saw that little black bag, sort of like the kind doctors used to carry, but smaller, I began to wonder does he have knives, or handcuffs, or some other kinky business. But he gives me two fifty-dollar bills and he tells me there are things his wife doesn't like to do and he goes around and around and what he's talking about is a blow-job, see. Plain and simple. But he's going on and on about it like it's the end of the world or something. But we finally get that out of the way and I go in the bathroom to gargle with the stuff I carry and when I come out again, oh-oh, he's got that little black bag on the bed and he's opening it. I'm edging toward the door, smiling, see, when he pulls this book out of the bag. A Bible. So help me Jesus, Mr. Benny, it was a Bible. A beat-up old Bible. And he asked me to get down on my knees with him, which I did, him being between me and the door, and he read out loud for a couple of minutes. He had a really nice voice. He wasn't reading real loud or crazy; it sounded real nice. And then we stood up, and I picked up my purse and the paper I had bought in the lobby while I was waiting for the right time to go up to the room. He took the paper out of my hand and looked at the front page, which had a big picture of that gook's finger in the plastic bag. And he said something funny, which has stuck in my mind ever since. He said, 'If you cut off their trigger fingers, they can't shoot no white Christian boys.' Something like that. I was around him by the door then, and I just left. Opened the door and left. He could have the paper, and welcome to it."

She took another sip of coffee.

I stood up and retrieved her coat from the back of the chair and held it while she slipped into it.

"Thank you for coming," I said. "I really appreciate it."

She turned around and put her arms around my neck, and before I could move, her lips were pressed to mine again. The way my reflexes were working, a second-grader could take away my lollipop in the schoolyard. I looked into her wide-open eyes and saw that they were narrowed a bit. The bitch was testing me. I laughed, which broke the contact.

"Anytime you change your mind, I'll be there, Mr. Benny," she said. "Anytime."

I walked her down to the door and asked if she wanted a cab. She thought for a second.

"No," she said, "it's early. I think I'll try these clothes out."

I took the coffee cups and the glasses into the kitchen, washed and dried them. I thought how Cathy would have laughed over what had happened. Maybe she *was* laughing. Maybe my father was playing the violin. Maybe the cow was jumping over the moon.

If you cut off their trigger fingers, they can't shoot no

white Christian boys. Or something like that. Something like what?

I got up about one A.M. and took one of Doc's pills, but it didn't work. So I did enough push-ups to make the smell of Darlene's perfume disappear. I first started doing push-ups on a regular basis when I was eleven years old to build up my upper body. Lately I'd been doing them to plug up my nose. What would you list that under in an exercise program?

8

There are all kinds of things you can do when a case turns cold. Of course, the case was cold when I got it, but I hadn't been able to warm it up to the temperature of the captain's left tit.

What you can do is lie doggo, going through a few motions at the office, but basically hiding out at your house, the gun range, a few quiet bars, or if you're a lover, going berserk during the day with waitresses who work at night or with unhappy or unfulfilled wives. The last two may sound redundant, but they're not. I once asked a lady with whom I was playing house to leave that house and move into mine, and she was shocked, absolutely shocked. And when she got through telling me how much she loved her husband, we did it one more time. Not for the Gipper, but just because she loved doing it one more time. She was just unfulfilled.

You can also ask to be taken off the case so that maybe someone new can come up with a fresh lead, which is what the captain was trying to do with Moran and me, but that hadn't worked this time either.

Or you can stay in there humping in the hopes that you'll stumble on something new or that something old will suddenly make sense, or that somebody's canary will suddenly sing something into somebody's ear, or that somebody somewhere will nab somebody else who will want to confess to the particular crime you are investigating.

I was humping. Except that I was just about all humped out. Doc had insisted I come home to dinner with him, and Doris Wallace had filled me so full of roast beef and mashed potatoes that I had an old-fashioned bellyache by the time I left their house about 8:45 P.M.

I sat in the car a few minutes thinking about their gratitude and how nice it was to be able to do something for people like that. Maybe I should take my six million and go around doing good. Ho ho ho, everybody, it's Santa Benny. Except that whenever people on television got a sudden windfall, it screwed up their lives worse than ever. I would have given a thousand dollars to be able to break wind at that moment, but God wanted me to suffer with all my money.

I turned on the radio and drove around the streets for a while, hoping in the back of my mind that I would hear a call on a robbery in progress or policemen needing help, but everything was either routine or in a district far away. I felt fat and bloated and useless and lonely, and I could feel my hands gripping the wheel with a force far beyond what was necessary to control the car.

When I pulled in to the curb and turned off the motor, I wasn't too surprised to find myself right outside the Dienben car lot. Here's where both crimes had taken place, and if the criminal didn't return to the scene of the crime, then it was the detective's job to do so.

I walked up to the fence and peered in, checking the neat rows of cars in the spotlights that shone down from the tall corner poles. Mrs. Dienben said her husband often came alone late at night to show a car to somebody who worked the third shift at a factory or if a couple worked different shifts and that was the only time they could get together. But there had been no record of him seeing anybody the night he was killed. The same was true of the missing son.

My gun was in my hand by the time I sensed the reason for its being there. Somebody was coming from between the second and third line of cars, and I crouched down to make myself as small a target as possible. When I recognized by the shape that it was Mrs. Dienben herself, I stood up and heard her give a little gasp as I did so.

"It's Sergeant Freedman," I said. "Is everything all right?"

"Oh, yes, Sergeant. I didn't know it was you."

"Are you here alone?"

"Yes. The accountant needed some figures, and I was in the office."

"You shouldn't be here alone. Your son or—"

"I suppose you are right, but it was something that came up late, and I just had to go check on a car in the lot before entering it in the book. Would you like some tea? I brought a big thermos with me."

She unlocked the door in the gate before I opened my mouth to answer, and I walked through as she secured it again. I followed her to the shed, where there were all kinds of papers spread out on one of the desks. She motioned me to a chair and picked up a large thermos, but just before she unscrewed the cap, she paused.

"I have a better idea," she said. "Please come."

She took a ring of keys off one of the hooks and went out the door with the thermos. I followed her to a corner of the lot, where she stopped in front of a huge van and unlocked the door. She reached inside and flicked a switch, which turned on a fluorescent light in the van, and motioned for me to enter.

It was incredible. The compartment was like the living room of an expensive house, with a large sofa and three easy chairs, wall-to-wall carpeting, small windows with closed venetian blinds, and cabinets that could conceal a bar or a television set or both.

"I told my husband he was crazy when he bought two of these, because they were so expensive," she said, "but he sold one to a church and now we have a business that is interested in this one to use it to transport executives to and from the airport so they can hold conferences on the way. It will be much more comfortable to take tea here."

She slid open a cabinet, and sure enough it was a built-in bar from which she removed two glasses. She poured the dark, steaming liquid into low highball glasses and handed me one with a smile. She would have made a hell of a stewardess.

"Did you come here for some particular reason?" she asked, her eyes focused on me for any sign of encouraging news.

"No," I answered, my hands around the glass in an attempt to get some warmth in that region to match the sudden cold in my belly. "I was just wandering around town and I ended up here. I don't know why. Frustration, maybe. To tell you the truth, Mrs. Dienben, I'm not getting anywhere. I can't seem . . . I can't . . ."

My eyes welled up with tears, and I looked at her, unable to understand what was happening to me.

"Come here, please," she said, patting the sofa

seat beside her, and when I didn't move, she stood up, took my hand, and led me over to the sofa, where she sat down beside me.

"You've got to let go, Sergeant," she said. "You've got to let go. Your wife is gone, just as my husband is gone. Forever. But life goes on and we must go on with it. You must break through to the other side."

She stood up and walked over to the door through which we had entered and pushed the button down in the lock position. Then she flicked the light switch with the tip of her finger and I caught the flash of red on her nail just before total darkness engulfed us. In a few seconds her hands encircled my head, and her lips were all over my face—kissing, sucking, licking—then her fingers moved over my body, as if she were memorizing a map for future reference.

My surprise was such that I was somewhat repelled by the wetness of what she was doing. It wasn't that it was something new. There were times when Cathy and I had practically smeared each other with saliva and times when we were bone dry with each other, each experience different in every way every time. I had been with a great many women before I met Cathy and I am positive that she had many, many men before me, but the first time with her had been a revelation, I think, for each of us, and each time after that was equally exciting and fulfilling. I don't know what it would have been like if we had been granted years and years together, and now I would never know, but right then I didn't feel that I wanted to break through to the other side.

Mrs. Dienben pulled back for a few moments and I heard the rustle of silk before she straddled me again, and a firm breast was pushed into my face, the hard nipple first in my right cheek and then moved over to my lips, which parted at its insistence. My left hand instinctively raised and cradled the other breast, the smoothness of the skin almost unreal to my fingertips.

Her hand took mine and led it down to her wetness and I knew I was lost even as she was unbuttoning and pulling and tugging, and our arms and legs went through the awkward gyrations and our bodies grunted and sweated their way through to three or four climaxes for her and one for me.

When she rolled off and disappeared in the darkness, I lay there and compared her to those who had come before. Cathy and I were in a league by ourselves; Mrs. Dienben was only in the second or even third rank of all the others. So much for Oriental art.

"Sergeant," said her voice from somewhere near my right ear, "was it good for you?"

I did not laugh. "Madam," I said, "you have helped me through to the other side."

I could hear silk rustling again and was wondering where my pants and other accoutrements were when she suddenly started to dress me in the dark, including the buttoning. I realized we were not going to have any light in there until we were both properly attired.

As my right hand was raised to accommodate my shirt sleeve, I smelled the lady on my fingers and brought the sharp aroma close to my nose. The squat Polish face of Sergeant Czarnecki at the firing range suddenly appeared before me.

"Remember," I heard his voice say, as he did every year when the new batch of rookies came to practice, "this is your society finger and this is your trigger finger. One is to play with and one is to kill with."

Trigger finger. *If you cut off their trigger fingers, they can't shoot no white Christian boys.*

"Mrs. Dienben," I said into the dark, "did you say your husband sold one of these vans to a church?"

"Yes," she said.

"Would that be on the list that Sergeant Moran had?"

"I am sure."

"Would you know the name of that church?"

"Yes. It is called the Church of the Holy Avenger."

"And who bought the vehicle for the church?"

"There were three of them."

"Which one was the minister?"

"They were all ministers."

"Was there one who seemed to be in charge?"

"Yes."

"Do you know his name?"

"No, I do not remember it."

"Do you remember what he looked like?"

"An imposing man. A big man."

"How old?"

"My husband's age."

"What color hair?"

"Silver. Silver white."

"And his voice?"

"Deep. An imposing voice."

"Would you have his name on your records?"

"Oh yes. He signed. He signed the check."

When I asked no more questions, she turned the light on. My clothes were all on my body, but were in disarray. She looked impeccable, not a hair out of place, not a trace of sweat. But there was a different look on her face. In an American, I would have called it a look of satisfaction. In a Vietnamese, I don't know.

"I hope I have helped you this evening, Sergeant," she said.

"Oh, yes, madam," I said, getting to my feet, "you have helped tremendously."

"I will continue to help you all I can," she said, "on every occasion."

"Thank you, madam," I said, escorting her back to the office. "But I really think you shouldn't come here alone at night."

"Your word is my command," she said. "I will go home now and finish in the morning."

"I need the name of the minister first."

"Ah, yes."

She pulled a book toward her and ran her finger down the line while my heart rate increased proportionately. Thankfully, it did not stop when she did.

"Barrow," she said. "The Reverend Clive M. Barrow."

"Do you have an address for the church?"

"Twelve-sixty-four Mullaney Drive."

"Did the other men sign?"

"No. That is the only name we have. Why do you wish to know this? Does it signify?"

"I don't know yet. I'll know more tomorrow."

"Do you wish more tea?"

"No! No, thank you. I have had sufficient."

I escorted her to her car and we bade each other very formal good-nights.

By the time I reached home I was so tired that I just dropped my clothes on the floor and crawled into bed without even brushing my teeth. As I tucked my hand under my cheek on the pillow, I smelled her aroma again. I thought of Cathy and how she would have laughed like hell at what happened to me. At least I think she would have. For the first time in I don't know how long, I slept like a log all the night through.

9

Moran had not signed out but was nowhere to be found in the building the next morning, and if I hadn't bumped into Perkins coming out of the interrogation room, it might have been another day down the drain.

"He's at that bar," said Perkins. "Christ, he practically lives there."

"Which bar?"

"The one where the fag got knocked off."

"He hasn't cleaned that up yet?"

"The sisterhood has closed ranks. They've got him walking up the wall."

Perkins gave me directions to the Limp Richard, which turned out to be one of those narrow entrances with no sign anywhere, just the street number, and the front window painted black. The door was locked at that time of morning, but I just banged away on it until finally I heard a bolt turn and a sour little face with a wispy blond mustache peered through the crack in the door and asked me what I wanted.

"I want Sergeant Moran if he's here," I told him in a cop voice.

The door opened and I followed the skinny little thing, who was wearing a frilly apron, through the dim recesses until we came out in a large room with a bar that ran along one side, booths around three sides, and a small dance floor in the middle. Moran was sitting in one of the middle booths on the far wall, slumped in the seat, staring at nothing. His pad and pencil were on the table before him, but the page was blank. I dropped down in the pew seat across from him. I was sure he had been aware of my presence from my first entrance; he was too good a cop to miss anything, even when he was comatose, but he chose not to even blink hello. I decided there was no use in going through the amenities.

"Did you check out every car that Dienben sold?" I asked.

He looked at me for a long second, decided not to talk, and just nodded.

"What about the luxury van?"

I could see him sifting through his mind; it was like watching the windows on a slot machine. He decided to speak.

"What luxury van?"

"The one the church bought."

There was some more sifting.

"Oh yeah. I remember. Lot of money for a van."

"Did you check them out?"

The head started to nod, but he couldn't push it hard enough to get it all the way down. The lie came too hard to this man. He started to bluster it out, but he couldn't even manage that very well.

"Christ," he said, "it's a church. I figured . . ."

I stood up.

"Thanks," I told him. "What's your problem here?"

"I've got it narrowed down to one," he said, "but I'm missing a piece that the D.A.'s going to want.

And they've shut down on me. I should have hit harder when they were all shook up. But I let it get away and now it may be too late."

"I heard there were four maybes."

"Yeah, but only one's got the makings."

"Why don't you bring all four in, and we'll give them the routines individually? Give your hot one to the captain, and the rest of us will work on the bridesmaids. We'll break somebody."

His head came up and he almost smiled.

"Jesus," he said, "that might work. I thought this was going to be a piece of cake, but nothing has been breaking right. That might work."

He started scribbling notes in his book as I walked from the room. There were guys on the squad who got their rocks off interrogating homosexuals. One of the strange things about the captain was that he never allowed any rough stuff. But when a foul-breathed detective sticks his mouth a quarter-inch from your nose and screams obscenities until your eyeballs revolve, that's usually rough enough to make a construction worker beg to confess. Maybe nothing would come out of the mass interrogation with each pair of detectives trying to convince each isolated suspect that his buddy in the next room was ratting on him, but at least it would get Moran out of his doldrums. I owed him that much.

The city map-guide in my car showed that Mullaney Drive was in the northeast section in an area I remembered as sparsely settled. The houses were mostly square boxes, and the church, which was a cinder-block building, had two mobile homes parked in the dirt parking lot in the back.

The plain sign on the brown grass in the front showed that it was the Church of the Holy Avenger and that the Reverend Clive M. Barrow was senior minister. It also said that there were services Tuesday nights at 7:30, so I put my foot on the gas pedal and eased away down the road in the hopes that nobody had noticed my curiosity. Maybe my mind was clicking too far ahead of what might actually be the case, but I could feel the adrenalin working through my body and when I got to the end of the street and pulled into a driveway so that I could turn around, I punched my fist as hard as I could against the padding on the dashboard, and then did it again before twisting the wheel and driving off.

The dull ache in my wrist felt good, but not good enough, so I slapped the red light on the roof of the car, turned on the siren, and drove back to the south side of the city fast enough to scare the hell out of at least three drivers on the way. I turned off the noise, retrieved the light from the roof, and pulled over to the curb. Maybe I should go somewhere and look up the Church of the Holy Avenger and the Reverend Clive M. Barrow. The thought of going through newspaper clips or city directories or the computer file at headquarters was squashed before it got to the front of my brain. Or the rear or wherever the hell it had to go to get me to move in that direction.

I put the car in gear and drove calmly through the streets until I reached the Dienben house. She was probably at the car lot. I rang the bell and ten seconds later she opened the door, looked at me, and stood aside so that I might enter.

She was wearing one of those long Vietnamese dresses. Black. With a slit in the middle that ran almost all the way up to her crotch so that when she moved, even the slightest, her bare bowed leg showed creamy against the black.

She motioned with her hand that I was to go into

the living room, and as I was moving, she started shouting loudly in Vietnamese, her beautiful face twisted strangely with the force of what she was saying.

One daughter ran out of the kitchen immediately, and within five seconds the other daughter ran down from upstairs. When they saw me, they bowed slightly to acknowledge my presence and then turned their attention to their mother, who was going at it a mile a minute. They both left the hallway and returned wearing light coats. Without looking at me, they went out the front door and closed it very quietly behind them.

I started to go all the way into the living room, but Mrs. Dienben scurried after me and took my hand. She led me up the stairs and into a large bedroom that was decorated in various shades of blue. The sun was streaming through one of the windows, and she pulled down the shade to mute the rays and then pulled the shade on the window of the adjoining wall. Each of her movements was so slow, so studied, that I could feel my heart slow in response and the muscles of my body loosen in soft ripples like on a pond where somebody has tossed in a pebble far on the other side.

She walked over and smiled up at me before removing my jacket and everything else I was wearing, each as an individual task, each hung carefully on a chair. She rolled back the covers from the bed and placed me in the middle. Then, as I watched, she slowly pulled the long gown over her head and then stood naked before me for a full minute, her eyes half-closed, her thoughts her own. She went to the bureau and opened a drawer from which she removed a bottle. Dermassage. Jesus. I was expecting myrrh and incense at the least, but there was nothing wrong with the Dermassage as she started at my neck and went over my whole body, fingertips, toes, and, finally, yes, right there.

By the time I went into her, or she into me, or whatever the hell we did, I was ready to fuck an entire continent, and it wasn't until several hours later that I looked around for a clock. The little radio by the side of the bed said it was 6:15 P.M.

"I must go," I said, swinging my legs over the side.

"The children will not be home until I call the office," she said.

"I must go."

"It is late. Let me make you food."

"No, thank you. I must go."

"You are going to work?"

"To church."

"To church?"

"To church."

"Ah. You feel better?"

"Much better. Much, much better."

"I can do anything more for you?"

"I would like to take a fast shower."

"I will soap you and scrub you with brush."

When I got in the car and started it up, just before I threw it into gear I punched the dashboard again as hard as I could. I don't know whether it was in disgust or relief or whether I just wanted to make myself realize that dead was dead and I was alive. Whatever it was, the fogginess was gone and I was myself again. Which may or may not have been the best way to be when you were on your way to church.

10

The parking lot was half-full of cars, or to be more specific, quarter-ton and half-ton trucks, nearly all of which were four-wheel-drive. The twin to the van in the Dienben car lot was parked on the edge of the sidewalk leading to the rear door of the church, and it took me a few moments to decide whether to go in that way or walk around to the front. Always take them from the rear, I would like to think my grandmother used to say, so I followed her advice and came through a classroom with chairs for little people and a chalked message on the blackboard that said something about it sometimes being necessary to die for Jesus just as he did for you. California probably has more kooky churches per square inch than any other state in the union. There is a church to fill every need or desire, ranging from group fucking to vomiting the evil from your body and soul. You could worship hard or soft. This seemed to be one of the hard ones. These people obviously didn't fool around even in kindergarten.

I passed a man and a woman on the stairs who stood aside and looked at me curiously but didn't say anything, and eventually reached the front hallway that was lit by a single hundred-watt bulb that hung naked on a metal chain.

The church part wasn't any fancier. There were rows of gray metal folding chairs, enough to hold maybe two hundred more than the sixty who were sitting bunched up near the front. In front of the chairs was a plain wooden platform raised a foot from the floor, and toward the front of it a lectern, and back of that a big, tall man holding a beat-up black Bible. A big, tall man with silver hair. Late forties, maybe early fifties. And when he saw me standing in the doorway, he said, "Come in, brother, come in. Join the throng right down front here."

And while I was taking my seat beside a guy in a red-checked shirt whose arms were as thick as my thighs, I thought to myself that if anybody had asked me how the preacher's voice sounded, I would have immediately replied that it was imposing.

"What is the voice of God?" he asked imposingly. "How does God speak to us from the heavens? Through thunder, right? God's voice is not a namby-pamby whine like one of those homosexuals. When God speaks through his thunder, you pay attention. Everybody pays attention. Because where there is thunder, there can also be lightning. And when God throws them bolts around, you pay closer attention. Because any minute, any second, one of those bolts can come straight for you. You! You might think you've covered up your sins, that nobody has noticed, that you've fooled your neighbors, your friends, even your husband or your wife. But God knows. God knows when you've sinned. And at this very moment he might be putting your name on one of his thunderbolts, and next thing you know, your brains are on fire as the lightning goes through you and turns you into ash. From dust to dust, the good book says. It's not talking about dying. There ain't no dying when you believe in Jesus. The Bible's talking about sin and what the lightning can do to you.

"My friends, the world today is rotten to the core. Rotten. It's been taken over by the liberals, the homosexuals, the Jews who betrayed Christ to his death on earth, the drunks, the fornicators, the cowards, the pissants who want to get down on their knees before the Communist atheists and beg them not to hurt them. Every day it gets worse and worse as the government squeezes you dry of your hard-earned money and tells you that you can't do this and you can't do that while the criminals roam the streets, the drug addicts, the junkies, the wet-backs, the scum of the earth roam free while the government turns the other cheek. There was a time in this country when the government was the friend of the people, when it protected right-thinking people rather than the criminal element, but those days are over. As you all know, the Lord helps those who help themselves, and we are prepared to help ourselves. When the time comes, when that big bomb goes off or when the Commies make their move to take over the world, the whole world, this little church is going to be ready. We are ready now. Through your hard work and sacrifices and donations and pitching in, we are ready. And we are also committed. We are committed to surviving, to seeing it through, to being there when the trumpet blows and the Lord tells us it is time to take over, to start again, to see to it that this time around the world gets off on the right foot with the right people, and that . . ."

At first I didn't know what it was about the congregation in the hall that set me on edge, that made me sit there with my fingers slipped into the opening of my jacket, three inches from my gun.

I've been in bars where I knew that every person present was capable of killing me if the opportunity presented, in alleys where death could appear from any window, in car chases where one little wrong twist of the wheel or one car coming out of nowhere could turn your body into raw meat, and I had to keep a tight asshole on each and every occasion. But these people were something beyond that. In the book, they were without doubt all solid American citizens—jobholders, deerslayers, housewives, voters, the works—but they also obviously had grave reservations about the way things were being done in our country and the world at large. The man up there on the podium was talking the millennium, Armageddon, tearing it all down to build it all over again. And the thing that bothered me, that set these people against everybody I had ever encountered before, was that they were not moving a muscle, not blinking an eye, barely breathing if at all. They were stone. Granite. There were no amens, no hands raised in the air, no souls displayed on the faces the way you see on television when the revival ministers are giving a football stadium full of sinners what-for.

These people were like a company of commandos, Green Berets, rangers, kamikazes, those guys who have been trained to the point of no return and are just waiting for the word to go ahead. All the men and women and the few kids who were there were exactly the same. Even the goddamned kids looked programmed.

I didn't know how or why the Reverend Barrow had killed Troo Song Dienben or what they had done with the part formerly attached to the finger of his son Troc, but I was positive I had come to the right place and had put the finger on the right man. As he went on about the evils of everybody but his own little band of brothers, I tried to figure how best to handle the particulars of the case. The district attorney's office was very demanding about particulars before an indictment was made and a person brought to trial. There was still a lot of investigating to do before charges could be brought and an arrest made. And even if I had a picture of whatever happened, and the strangling wire and the bolt cutters, I wasn't about to tackle this crowd on my own. The guy sitting on my left could have compressed me into a dumpling with just one ripple of his arm.

The sermon went on for another thirty-five minutes, with the Reverend Barrow going over basically the same ground from little different angles, his voice soothing enough so that you went into a semidream state, and I started thinking about Mrs. Dienben and the afternoon and how stupid I had been to underrate her abilities and that maybe I should stop by to see her on the way home in case anything new had developed while I was in church. I hadn't had any lunch and there had been no time for dinner and maybe we could go out and get something to eat and then I could show her my apartment, which she had never seen.

It wasn't until people started rising around me that I realized the services were over, and I thought how strange it was that there were no hymns or passing of the basket or any of the other things I associated with church services.

I was following the crowd out the front door, noticing how little talk there was among them, and just as I reached the hallway, a great big guy I had not noticed before took hold of my arm.

He was dressed in a dark suit that was off the rack from some discount house, with a white shirt and a plain black tie. On his feet were what had to be logger's boots, and I wondered how high they came up his leg under his pants. He looked like a nine-incher to me.

"Excuse me, sir," he said, "but the Reverend Barrow would like a word with you in his office."

"I'll have to come back for that," I told him. "I have a previous appointment." He was not letting go of my arm. I thought of shrugging his hand off or even violently shaking it off, but this guy was big and I decided to wait it out.

"It will only take a moment of your time, sir," he replied in the patient voice of a very strong man.

Now was the time to make the move while the people were still there, but even as I thought it, I knew they were no factor in the event. This guy could pull out a gun and shoot me dead and there would be no reaction from this crowd. I allowed him to gently pull me back into the room where the services had taken place and then through a metal door at the left rear.

The room was about twelve by twelve with a wooden desk and a filing cabinet and four of the same gray folding chairs as the only furniture. The reverend was sitting behind the desk on one of the chairs, and standing against the wall was what could have been the twin of the behemoth who had brought me there.

"Good evening," said the reverend. "We are always interested in newcomers to our little church. What is your name and what was it that brought you here tonight, friend?"

I had my gun but the big guy was two inches from me with both eyes peeled. By the time I could snake my hand into my jacket, he could have broken the arm into two separate pieces. And then the guy on the wall could have peeled my fingers off one by one. I could have lied about my name and tried to bluster it through, but there was my wallet and identification. The only thing that could get me out of there was truth. Well, partial truth, anyway.

"My name is Benjamin Freedman," I said, "and I am a sergeant in the police department. I heard about your church from another policeman. I have not been a regular churchgoer, but I recently lost my wife, and I have been looking around to join a church to help me through my difficult time."

"Freedman," echoed the reverend, "Benjamin Freedman. That ain't no Christian name. Seems to me you would be checking out synagogues and suchlike."

He drawled out the word "synagogue" so that it sounded like "syna*gawwwg*."

"My wife was a Christian," I said, "and we had discussed religion in great detail before she died, and I am looking to find some way to be close to her again."

"So you came here to our little church to seek your salvation," he said with a smile. "Now, ain't that nice. Ain't that nice, reverend?" he asked, turning his head to the lunk who was standing right beside me. The guy never moved a muscle. "Ain't that nice, reverend?" he asked the guy against the wall, who never took his eyes off me for a second.

"Well," he said to me, the only one seemingly paying attention, "I think that's nice. And maybe we can do something to help you. As a matter of fact, we have a church camp out in the country a ways, and we are having a special meeting there this very night. You can come along and see how this church operates, and maybe we can help you find your way to Jesus."

"Oh, I couldn't come tonight," I told him. "I

have to report for duty in half an hour. I told them I was coming here to attend the service and then would report right to work. If I don't get there on time, they will send a squad car to see what's holding me up."

"Well then," said the reverend, standing up, "I guess it will have to be another time. Too bad. I think you'll like our little camp. We have all the conveniences out there. We have both Saturday and Sunday services out there if you'd care to come again."

"That sounds fine," I told him. "Probably Saturday. Or Sunday, if I can't make it on Saturday."

I knew I was babbling away, but I was scared, deep down, and all I could think of was getting out that door, into my car, and back to civilization.

As I was talking, I was moving, and I had my hand on the knob and was turning the handle when I felt the blow on the back of my head that knocked me into the door and out cold. I don't know when the signal was given or whether it was a fist or a club from behind, but either way it did the trick. And as I was falling to the floor and blacking out, I had just time to wonder whether I had finally come to Jesus after all.

11

The naked light bulb hanging from the ceiling fooled me into believing that I was still in the church, and I lay still for a few moments trying to think of what I could say to these guys that would get me off the hook and out of there. But when I realized that I wasn't on the floor, that I was lying on a bare mattress on a narrow cot in a concrete room with a metal door and no windows, my stomach contracted violently over and over again, as though it were intestinal hiccups.

I have learned to live with fear. I had worked out ways to compensate for the sudden rushes of adrenaline that go through my body whenever danger seems imminent or when I am actually under attack. My father was one of those "Never again" Jews who took no shit from anybody on any occasion. Whatever the Israelis did, whether it was invading Lebanon or annexing the West Bank or blowing the Iraqi nuclear reactor to tiny atoms or getting up in the United Nations and telling the Russians to go fuck themselves, it was fine with him. Two thousand years was too long to keep turning your cheeks, he said. Show them the cheeks of your ass, and then blow one at them.

My mother was the same about her side. She had a brother in the IRA who was gunned down by the

British when he tried for some unknown drunken reason to wipe out a police station all by himself, and whenever she was in her cups, she would pull me to her flat bosom, tears falling all over my face, and make me promise that I would never forget that I came from a family of fighters, men who had the courage to risk their lives for "the cause."

There was also my paperback book. I never knew the name of it or who wrote it because the cover and the first two pages had already been ripped off by the time I came across it. But it was about World War II and the Germans and the Americans, especially an American Jew who got killed fighting the Nazis. And there was a passage in the book where a Gestapo officer was questioning a Frenchman, and the Nazi told the Frenchman that if he didn't talk, he was going to rip his eyeball out. Which he did. Plunged his finger into the socket and ripped out the eyeball.

And I made up my mind, was I nine or ten years old, that nobody would ever beat me to the punch, that I would do anything and everything I had to in order to keep me going, that if anybody's eyeballs were going to be ripped out, they were going to be somebody else's eyeballs.

That summer when my father was playing at Tanglewood, he sent me to sports day camp because by that time my mother barely got out of bed anymore, and on the second day I ran into two guys who thought it was funny to keep pounding on my arms. It took two counselors and three campers to pull me off them, my internals driving me so hard that they couldn't handle my arms and legs and head and teeth without getting bitten or scratched or belted. I did the same thing when I went through the martial-arts phase in high school. Somebody would knock me on my ass, and I would go berserk until the instructors would jump in and pin me to the mat.

One day the head instructor called me in his office and said I would have to quit unless I learned to control my temper. "The force you have inside you is good," he said, "but it must be controlled in order to be useful."

He was the one who taught me how to breathe, how to calm my body when the juices wanted to drive themselves right out the top of my skull. It had worked through all my years of police work, whether it was neutralizing a recalcitrant prisoner or shooting it out with junkies in a liquor-store heist. First the wild burst of energy, then the fake calm. Both the people on the street and the cops I worked with learned to give me room. And when everything else failed, there were always my push-ups.

But here I was so scared that I couldn't stop my stomach from shaking. I put both hands flat over my belly button, hoping to bring warmth to the center, breathed deep and slow, closed my eyes and sought the blankness, but it wouldn't come. Somebody had me buried in concrete, and any minute they could be coming in for my eyeball.

It is impossible to tell time when you are trapped in a tomb in which you hear no sound except the rapid beating of your own heart. So it could have been a minute or an hour or a day later when there was a clank outside and the door was pulled open. A woman came through it, a big woman. A big, good-looking woman. Somewhere in her middle thirties. Khaki shirt, khaki pants, a .37 magnum in a holster on her waist. Tied down. The holster was tied down.

She looked me over an inch at a time, her hands on her hips. A leader. You could tell that she was a leader of whatever the hell had to be led in wherever the hell I was.

"Well," she said, and you knew from just that one word that this lady was about as Southern as they can go in the swamps below the Mason-Dixon line, "you finally woke up. This is the third time I've come down to welcome you to camp. Even squeezed your pecker once, but it didn't even make you breathe hard. The Reverend Philip must have laid it on you good."

"I think I hit the door on the way down," I told her, not wanting the baboon to get too much credit. Jesus. I had to act macho even about getting knocked out. What the hell difference did it make whether he could hit that hard? Was I trying to whistle my way past the graveyard? He ain't so much, lady. Bring him around again and let him try it when we're face to face. Then see what happens. Deep down I knew. He'd hit me hard enough in the front to drive the back of my head into the wall this time. And here I was trying to convince her that I'd been done in by a door. She wasn't paying attention anyway.

"We've been checking you out," she said. "Newspapers say you're the detective looking into the killing of that gook car dealer. Why'd you come sniffing around our church?"

"My wife died recently," I said, "and I've been—"

"Heard that story already," she said quickly. "My husband told me all that. I came down here to get the real story, the true story. Why'd you come sniffing around our church?"

"My wife died," I said, "and this policeman I work with told me that . . ."

She pulled the gun from the holster, reversed it in her hand, and smashed me on the temple with the barrel. I watched her face as she was doing it, never dreaming what the end result was going to be, and there was just the tiniest hint of a smile on her lips just before the blackness wiped out her and everything else. It was as if she had come in there with the intention of whacking me with her gun, and things had gone just the way she had hoped. No matter what I had told her, the end result would have been the same. And while that was going through my mind, I was wondering which one was her husband. Barrow? Phil? Or the one leaning against the wall?

When I came to the next time, the boss man himself was looking down on me, with the Reverend Phil about two steps behind.

"My wife says she had a little talk with you," he said, answering one of my questions, "and you didn't give very satisfactory answers."

"Do you have any idea what kind of trouble you people are in?" I asked him, the pain in my head vibrating through my whole body. "You have kidnapped a policeman and caused him bodily harm. Before this goes any further and more people get involved, you better get me to a phone so I can call the department, and then we'll go in and try to straighten some of this out."

"Come on," he said, "let's not waste any more time. Why don't we straighten it out here and now? I'm going to ask you one more time nice, and then I'm going to let Phil ask you mean. Why'd you come to our church?"

"I'm working on the Dienben killing."

"What's that got to do with our church?"

"You bought a van from him. I saw it."

"Hell, man, a lot of people must have bought cars from him. You checking all them out, too?"

"Yes."

"What?"

"We had no real leads. So we're checking out everybody who bought a vehicle there within the past six months."

"Jesus Christ Lord Almighty. So you didn't particularly think we had anything to do with it? You were just checking us out like everybody else?"

"Yes."

"And do you think we did it?"

"I don't know. I hadn't gotten very far. Did you do it?"

"Hell, no! Why would we want to kill that gook for?"

"You were there the night he was murdered." Jesus Christ! What the hell was the matter with me? Here I was completely at the mercy of these two apes, and I was slipping in a trap line from an interrogation, just as though we were in the station house and I was holding all the cards. Habits die hard. And you could also die hard from a habit.

"We were there to have the transmission checked. He said it was just a little tight during the break-in period and would ease out after a couple thousand more miles were put on it. And then we drove off."

"Well, if you had nothing to do with the killing and you are innocent in all respects, then you had better turn me loose before you get in real trouble. You made an honest mistake, and we'll take that into account, but this has gone far enough."

I rolled off the cot as slowly as I could, my head once removed from my body. The pains were shooting in and out from all sides, and when I put my hand up to various spots, all I could feel was sticky hair matted down in odd clumps.

They were watching me clinically, like somebody thinking of buying a horse or a cow at an auction in another county than their own.

"Is my car still in the lot?" I asked.

"It's here."

"In the church lot?"

"No, here."

"Where the hell is here?"

"At camp. We're at camp."

"What camp?"

"The church camp. I told you about that."

"Where is it? Where are we?"

"We're about twenty miles into the canyons."

"But my car's here?"

"It's here all right. Reverend Phil drove it out for you."

I gave him the best smile of appreciation I could under the circumstances, but he didn't smile back. The two of them followed me out the door at a leisurely pace, and we entered what appeared to be a small dormitory with double bunks against the walls, enough for twenty people. This was lit by two naked bulbs hanging from the ceiling, and there was another door against the opposite wall. Slow and easy, I was saying to myself as we walked across the room. Slow and easy, slow and easy. We walk out of here slow and easy, get into the car and drive off. My head hurt like hell.

I pulled open the metal door and entered into what seemed to be a cave with a square mouth leading to the sunlight that blinded my eyes after the dim interior. We came out to the canyon floor, and I could see cave mouths in all directions around me, holes in the stone cliffs, and there were also plain framed wooden buildings and a couple of log huts. There were seven or eight people moving about, all dressed in the same kind of khaki that Mrs. Barrow had worn. Most of them also had handguns belted on, and one of the men had an automatic rifle strapped across his shoulder. It looked like one of those camps in the South American jungle you see on television all the time where CIA-backed guerrillas train to destroy governments that have pissed off whoever holds the presidency of the United States at that particular point in time.

"On a weekday like this," Barrow said, "we're only able to maintain a bare muster for the essential services. But you'll see that on the weekend everybody pitches in to build the camp to what we're going to need for the Armageddon. When those great hailstones fall from the sky, if God don't level these mountains along with all the rest, we should be fine and dandy in the caves."

"You think God is going to go shazaam and blow us all to hell?"

"Through the bombs, son. Those bombs are going to do the trick for him."

"Is this one of those end-of-the-world churches where you set a day and all your people are going to come here to wait it out?"

"If God is good enough to reveal the day to me, I will call the flock. But more likely he's just going to let it happen, and those he has chosen to be saved will be saved, and those who are with sufficient sin he will let die."

"How do you think you'll make out personally, Reverend?"

He smiled at me. "His will be done," he said. "I ain't losing any sleep over it."

By this time we were in the center of the compound, but I couldn't tell which direction was out. Just as I was about to ask where my car was, two women carrying rifles came out of one of the cave mouths with a skinny kid wearing a bright yellow rain jacket just ahead of them.

As they came abreast of us, my stomach gulped,

the suddenness making my whole body shake. Here was the missing son of the Dienben family, and a quick glance at his right hand disclosed a fresh white bandage that covered the palm and the space where a finger should have been.

The dream world I had been walking in suddenly collapsed. The three of us had not been walking casually toward the parking lot somewhere so I could get into my car and drive back to my former life. These people were in control of my life, and as I panicked, I started running, heading toward what looked like a passage in the cliffs.

I could hear the Reverend Phil pounding after me and I was sure the women with the prisoner had lifted their rifles, so I started to zig and zag as I ran, each pound of my foot on the dirt reverberating in my head tenfold. And just as I was nearing the gap, out of one of the cave holes popped Mrs. Barrow, who threw a block into me that would have gotten her a lifetime contract with any team in the National Football League. I went down hard and stayed there, my whole body a shambles. She rolled and came up, her pistol drawn and pointed down at me. But when she saw that I was unable to move, she calmly flipped the gun in her hand and banged the barrel on my forehead once again.

"Armageddon," flashed through my mind as the light went out. "Armageddon."

12

At first I thought I was back in the same cave, but then I realized that the bed was different, a little bigger, and there was a sheet under me and a blanket over me, and there was an old-fashioned floor lamp along the wall to furnish a weak light that reflected dimly off the blue-painted walls. There were three other beds like mine in the room, but the mattresses were naked on these, with khaki blankets folded at the bottom of each mattress.

On a stool beside my bed was an orange plastic tray with a sandwich and a drink on it. The cheese was also orange, as was the drink, and the bread had started to curl up at the edges.

I wasn't hungry but my bladder was aching, and I looked around the room for whatever might be available. There was a beat-up old metal pail in the left corner, and I crawled out of bed and shuffled over to the pail and urinated myself back to bodily comfort. It was noisy as hell doing it in the metal pail, and I kept looking over my shoulder at the door in case somebody came through. There's no more helpless feeling in the world than to be caught in the middle of a piss.

My head felt like a boil looks, all puffed up, red and angry, full of a soggy white mass with just a hint of yellow in it. If I moved it too quickly or tried to turn it too far, the pain went right down through my neck into a sick feeling in the middle of my stomach. These people hit you on the head like McDonald's sells hamburgers.

A church camp. This was one hell of a church camp. Guns. Uniforms. And Troc Dienben. They were holding Troc Dienben minus one finger. As the man said, this must be the place.

The slam of a bolt being pulled back on the metal door was like a rifle shot going off, and I jumped to my feet from the cot, making my head spin in three different directions. Barrow came through the door shadowed by Phil and a moment later the Mrs. Just the sight of the lady made me pull my head down into my neck as far as it would go, but she paid me no mind as she walked over and sat down on one of the beds.

The Reverend Philip was carrying a wooden chair which he placed down beside my bed, and Barrow sank onto it and looked at me intently.

"Benny," he said gravely, "you are not cooperating with us at all. If you seriously intend to become a member of this church, then you have got to cease all your peckerwood activities and learn to cooperate. Now, why did you try to cut and run on us out there?"

"I saw the boy," I told him. "You had informed me that you had nothing to do with what happened to Mr. Dienben, and then I saw his son out there. You lied to me, and all of this will be taken into account when you are brought to trial."

The look on his face was almost painful as he listened to my words. What I was saying was obviously hurting his feelings. The weakness of my position in the situation was taking a toll on my body, and I could feel myself sagging on the bed, almost ready to curl into a fetal position and maybe stick my thumb in my mouth. I wondered if they had damaged some part of my brain, and looked reproachfully over at Mrs. Barrow, who was scratching vigorously under her large left breast. I noticed that my shoes were placed neatly under the bed on which she sat. Up until then I hadn't realized I wasn't wearing them. My head really hurt.

"Look, son," said Barrow, "the fate and weight of the entire world might be resting on our little brotherhood. We could be all that is left when the bombs go off. That is a tremendous responsibility, and we do not take it lightly. Every member of our church has pledged everything—body, soul, and worldly goods—to the Second Coming. We may be God's only fortress when the Devil makes his move."

"Then why the devil did you kill Dienben and then kidnap his son?" I yelled at him, the sound ringing in my ears like a brass gong.

Once again I got that patient look with the faint hint of hurt and reproach and just the touch of anger in it. This guy had to have taken lessons from the same drama teacher who coached President Reagan.

"I told you, son, and I'm telling you one last time. Nobody has killed nobody around here yet. There's going to be killing, you can bet on that, and you damned well might be the first one to go if you keep on like this, but we had nothing to do with what happened to the car dealer. We do have the boy; you saw him. But we took him for God's work. We need money for our mission. This whole parish sweats and strains and does their damnedest, but it's all they can do to keep their own lives going until the time comes, let alone the church and the camp here. You know how many people we got here right now? It's Wednesday. Everybody's got to be at work on Wednesday. Sure, they can come out on the weekends; we're garrisoned right to our asses on weekends. But on a weekday, there's us and maybe a couple of retirees and any of the women who don't have washing to do.

"We need money bad. You know how much gas that generator burns just to keep these few lights flickering? Our well ain't that good, and we got to go deeper. We need supplies and ammunition and some heavier weapons. We need money. We tried joining up with some of those other organizations. Hell, I wrote the Posse Comitatus, the Identity Church, and the American Tax Freedom Institute, thinking they might want to help a church like ours. Two of them didn't even answer and the other sent a form letter asking us for funds. *Us!* I thought we had a friend when I read about the Way International because they were training their people with guns, but when I wrote them about it, they wrote back to say they didn't use guns anymore, that their only weapon was the Word. Hell, I got all the words this bunch can use. It's guns we need. So I figured that once the furor dies down, we'll just write that gook lady a letter and tell her how much it is going to cost to get her son back. She's got lots of money now. You see all the cars in that lot? You know what we paid for that van? She's got lots of money."

"What kind of a church are you running?" I yelled at him. "What kind of a minister are you? What kind of a God tells you to kidnap people and hold them for ransom and beat up a cop and hold him against his will? What kind of a Christian builds a fort and buys guns and plans on killing people? This is crazy. Throw it all in before it's too late. Give me my goddamned shoes and let me take you in before they come in and bust you all up."

"Son," said Barrow, "you don't seem to understand your situation. We can't set you loose. We're committed. We're not going to stop or let anything get in our way. We're all God-fearing, law-loving people, but we have a mission that's bigger than me or my wife or any of the other reverends here. Bigger than you, son. We can't let you loose to tell your tale and have people trying to interfere with our mission before the time has come. You're a Jew; you people are smart. Especially at raising money. What would you do?"

I opened my mouth to answer him, but there was no answer. Of course he couldn't let me go. Both of us were smart enough to know that. What would I do if I were in his position? I'd kill me, that's what I'd do. Especially if I believed that God would approve of me doing just that in order to preserve his mission. If I looked at it logically, then I guess I was a dead duck.

"I've got some money," I said, moving my head around as I said it, so that everybody in the room clearly heard the statement.

"What's that, son?" asked Barrow, leaning forward in the chair a bit.

"I've got some money from my wife's insurance. It came to twenty-five thousand dollars, and I can get it in payments of five thousand dollars at a time."

"What do you mean, son?"

"It was set up so that I can get only five thousand dollars at a time. Then I have to wait a while before I can get another five thousand dollars. I would be happy to contribute some to the church for whatever might be needed."

"You would be willing to give us this money?"

"If it will help to prepare for the end of the world, then I think I should."

"How do you get this money?"

"All I have to do is call up a man and he will have the money delivered to me."

Mrs. Barrow stood up noisily from her bed and walked over to stand beside her husband's chair, her figure looming over me. Pulling her gun from the holster, she reversed it in her hand and squinted at my head. My hands started to move up my body, ready to form an X of protection for the much-abused cranium, and seeing that, she smiled her little smile, slipped the gun back in the holster, and returned slowly to her seat. Barrow and Phil had not stirred while this was going on, and there was no sound until she sat down again.

"You can get this money in cash?"

I nodded, not wanting to break the rhythm of his thoughts with sound.

"Well," said Barrow, standing up, "we'll have to get you to a phone."

"I can call right from here," I said.

"There's no phone here," said Mrs. Barrow. "We don't have any of what you'd call the modern conveniences. And I doubt you can reach your insurance company on the CB radio."

"No, I have to have a phone."

"We'll get you to a phone soon enough, friend," said Barrow. "Meanwhile, why don't you eat your nice sandwich and take it easy until we come back for you."

"Bolt's coming off that door," said Phil. He could talk. "Won't hold for beans 'less we get it welded."

Barrow thought for a moment. "Clara and Myrt have to get back to town," he said, "and we ain't got nobody else worth a damn. Lock him in with the Chinee boy for now."

And that's how I got to meet Troc Dienben.

13

The Reverend Phil took me to the new room all by himself, and even though he had no visible weapon, I didn't make any kind of a move. It wasn't only that he was at least five inches taller than my five-foot-ten, and was maybe fifty pounds heavier than my one hundred and sixty-five, and that he probably had a gun or a knife or a 105 mm. field piece concealed on his person somewhere. I was also still very weak from the pounding my head had taken from various and assorted persons, and it was all I could do just to place one foot in front of the other. The time they opened Cathy up to find out exactly how far the cancer had progressed, I had looked through the window into the operating room where the five people were clustered around her table, and I thought how odd it was that these five people were dealing with life and death while the rest of the world went about its business. Here I was penned up in a church camp with my life or death hanging in the balance, and part of the tiny group holding me consisted of two blue-collar wives who had to get back to town to put supper on the table for their families. Was Moran wondering where I was? The captain? Doc? My father used to say that's how it was with the Jews and the Nazis. The torturers knocked off for the day when it was time for supper with their families outside the concentration camps. Never again. Maybe yes never again, maybe no never again. But first I had to get my head together if it was going to be maybe yes.

The new place was a little side room deeper into the mountain off a main cave. There were two bolts on this narrow door, and when Phil got it open, I was surprised at just how small the area was, dimly lit by the kind of table lamp that kids make in manual-training class. The wire that gave it power came through a hole that had been drilled through the rock, and the lamp was the only piece of furniture in the room. Young Dienben was sitting on the floor with his back against the wall, and only his eyes moved as Phil pushed me gently through the door and then closed it on my back.

As soon as I heard the second bolt slide shut, I walked over and went down on one knee beside him.

"Troc?" I asked, following established procedure. His eyes stayed focused on my face, and I took this to be a positive response.

"I've come to get you out of here," I told him, and then I sank down on the cheeks of my ass and started to laugh.

"Yes," I said. "You're going to find this hard to believe, but I've come to get you out of here."

"Who are you?" he asked, reaching out with his unmangled hand as if I had come to bring him something to hold on to. He looked small for nineteen years old, and he smelled of fear, the rank, sour stink of fear that always brought me up short when I encountered it in the police station. There had been occasions when I had been responsible for causing that smell to rise out of people, and it always gave me a bad feeling in my gut and once in a while dreams that wouldn't go away even after I woke up. Sometimes I wondered why God didn't take all the people who caused fear and grind them into shit. And other times I knew why. Ask the members of the Spanish Inquisition. Ask the Nazis. Ask the good people of the church who had caused the fear in this young boy. Ask me.

"I'm Sergeant Freedman from the police department," I told him. "I've been working on who murdered your father and what happened to you, and I came across these people. Now I know that they killed your father and kidnapped you, but right now I'm not in a very good position to do anything about it. I've been with your mother . . . I have seen your mother, and everything is all right with the rest of your family. They're worried about you, but they are all right otherwise."

I knew I was babbling again, and I put my right hand up to check the state of my head, which was now fairly crusty in the spots that had been sticky.

"Is there anything sticking out of my head?" I asked Troc, turning it this way and that so he could see all sides.

"What?"

"Are there pieces of bone sticking out anywhere, or something that looks like it shouldn't be like that?"

He humored me by looking intently at my revolving skull, and then shook his own head. "It's bloody and dirty," he said, "but there's nothing weird."

"Your English is even better than your mother's," I told him.

"She taught us in the old country when we were kids," he said, "and I travel with a pretty cool crowd in town."

"What have you found out about this place since you've been here?" I asked.

"They cut off my finger," he said, holding up the bandaged hand.

"Who did it?"

"I don't know. They gave me a shot of something, and when I woke up there was a bandage on my hand and it hurt terrible. It itches now. The big lady changed the bandage and said it was doing all right. They cut off my finger because of my father. Next they will strangle me."

"No, no," I said. "They're after money. You're no good to them dead."

"No, they will strangle me because of my father. They have cut off my finger and next they will strangle me."

He was shaking against the wall as if he had flu symptoms and the stink was coming off him something fierce. I tried to figure out how many days he'd been cooped up in this hole, but my brain wasn't capable of handling figures. I was sure that a piece of bone had to be sticking out somewhere. How long was I going to last in there?

"Tell me about this place," I repeated, hoping to distract him a little and find out something at the same time. "How many caves are there? How many people? What kind of weapons do they have? What have you seen?"

"There are many caves and many rooms, and there are hidden passages between the caves. Two days ago, Ben, he's here all the time, had to check out the humidity level in some of the caves, and he brought me along with him. He's not a bad guy. He acts tough when the others are around, but he's been nice when we've been alone. The boss's wife is mean; she tried to hit me on the head with her gun, but she missed and cracked me on the shoulder. She showed me her tits when she was alone in here with me, and then she tried to crack me on the head. They're going to strangle me because of my father."

"Nobody's going to strangle you," I told him again. "They're holding you for ransom, and you'll either get out that way, or somebody is going to come and blow us out of here. Nothing to worry about. Tell me some more about the caves."

But before he could say anything, we heard the bolts being pulled back, and the door opened and in came an old guy, had to be around seventy, wearing the khaki fatigues and carrying a bolt-action Springfield rifle. It was all oiled up nice and shiny, but I recognized it from the police armory museum. Christ, how long ago had it been when I had to memorize all those guns and rifles? Too long to be cooped up in a cave with an old fart holding a Springfield rifle on me.

I came out of the crouch as hard as I could and took him right in the middle, slamming him against the rock wall with an oof that guaranteed unconsciousness if not death. And the goddamned rifle came out of his hands and the barrel belted me right across the head so hard that I heard the stars banging around inside my skull. I fell backward on my ass and was staring at the old man sliding down the side of the wall when through the door came the Reverend Phil and his buddy followed by Barrow. Phil's hand came out of nowhere to slam me in the chest with such force that I echoed the old guy's oof and fell back on the floor, the back of my head taking a terrible bang.

Phil reached down with his left hand, grabbed my jacket, and pulled me to my feet, his right hand cocking backward, the fist looking as big as a basketball.

"No," yelled Barrow, "I don't want him marked up any more. He has to make his call in town. You can do the other one."

The hand holding me went slack and I fell down to the floor again as Phil reached over and picked up Troc, held him for a moment, and then started smashing his face, fronthand and backhand, palm open, with such force that blood spurted from the nose and, I could swear, the ears and eyes.

I yelled and started to climb to my feet but the other ox shoved out his foot and trampled me to the floor again.

"He didn't do anything," I yelled. "It was me. Me. I'm the one hit the old guy. It was me. Leave him alone. It was me."

I don't know how long it went on before Barrow called out sharply, "Phil!" He didn't hear him and Barrow yelled again, "Phil. Phil. Phil."

The hand, red and dripping, stopped in midair, paused for a moment as though to continue, and then stopped and fell to the side. Phil held the boy for another moment and then opened his left hand and the body dropped just as I had, beside me, the face a red blotch. Phil stood there, body still as stone, moving breath in and out of his chest in gusts, not from the physical effort but as a means to control himself. The other guy took his foot off me and stepped back.

"Phil," said Barrow, "go get the van. We've got to take the Jew boy to town to make his call. You go get the van now."

Phil turned and walked out of the room without looking to right or left.

"Billy Bob," said Barrow, "you take Ben on up to

his room and make him comfortable, and then come on back here with my missus and a wet cloth to clean this boy up some. And a pillow and a blanket."

Billy Bob lifted old Ben easily and carried him out, Springfield rifle and all.

"This boy needs a doctor," I said. "He may be dying."

"He'll be all right," said Barrow. "He's breathing fine. Just be grateful he got what was meant for you. Once Phil gets his hormones going, it has to come out somewhere and you're lucky I was able to turn him on the boy. That could be you laying there just as easy as plum jam."

I looked down at Troc, who had bubbles of blood coming out of his mouth every time he took a painful breath. I had told him I was there to take him home, and because of me he had almost gone all the way home. Forever and ever.

"Soon as Billy Bob gets back," said Barrow, "we'll take us a little ride to the church and then you can call that insurance man about the five thousand dollars. We sure can use that money. Twenty-five thousand, your wife left you? Too bad you can only get it five thousand at a time. She didn't leave you any leeway for emergencies."

I started retching, my stomach heaving with fierce, grinding movement, but nothing would come up, and there I was on the floor like a dog, arms and legs spread out, gasping for whatever air I could get in between the spasms.

By the time they stopped, Billy Bob was back with a wet cloth, a pillow without a case, and a brown wool blanket.

"Missus said she'll be along when she can to fix him up," he said, dumping everything in a pile, the wet cloth on top of the pillow.

"Come along, boy," Barrow said to me, poking me with the toe of his cowboy boot.

Billy Bob lifted me to my feet and helped me out the door, waiting while Barrow threw the two bolts. With his help, I made it out the mouth of the cave. The sun had moved behind the cliffs and there was the pale reflection of twilight off the gray rocks. Time to go make that call. If I hadn't been able to think of Cathy's money, I'd either be already dead or maybe lying in that hole back there like Troc. Money is a mixed blessing, I'd like to think my grandmother might have said.

14

The church van was an exact duplicate of the one I had investigated with Mrs. Dienben, except that a picture of Jesus in his agony hung over the bar, and each of the other walls had crucifixes screwed into the wood.

Barrow sat in the back with me while Billy Bob drove. Phil had disappeared after removing the unconscious Ben from the cave. It could be that I had hit the old guy harder than I thought, and Phil and Mrs. Barrow were still taking care of him. I hoped someone was taking care of Troc.

My hands were linked behind my back by a pair of handcuffs of the type that had been declared obsolete by our force at least ten years before, but they were still adequate to their purpose. Billy Bob had also tied a piece of clothesline around my left leg, and Barrow held the other end loosely in his hand. He sat there with a five-thousand-dollar smile on his face, thoughts of twenty-five thousand obviously dancing through his brain.

"There's still time to get out of this," I said to him as the van started to roll forward. "Nobody is dead yet; I can still do you some good with a judge."

He beamed back at me, not even bothering to answer.

"What national church are you tied in with?" I asked.

This did strike a responsive chord because his face screwed itself up for a moment.

"We are the national church," he said, "and someday we'll have satellites all over the world. When I first started in this, when I decided to give up the bakery and found the church, I looked into affiliating with a national group, but the first two gave me a hard time about my reverency. They said I wasn't qualified according to their standards. Pissants. All of them."

"Where did you get your training?"

"Well, the missus and me read about all these people not paying taxes because they were ministers of God, and we sent away the money and got our diplomas from this church in San Diego, and then one night, must have been about three in the morning, I was shoving the bread into the oven, and there in the flames of the gas jets I saw the face of God, and I heard his voice say that I should take the loaves I baked and divide them up amongst the true believers in the world, that the bombs were coming and it was up to me to gather a flock and prepare for the end and a new beginning. So I sold the bakery and came out here to the place where our ministries had come from but they had moved without any forwarding address, and I started preaching in a storefront and pretty soon we had enough people to build our church and start the camp."

"How many parishioners do you have altogether?"

"We have sixty-six adult members, all good people, all ready to do what is necessary for the Second Coming."

"Do you really believe the world is coming to an

end, or is this just a gimmick for you to bullshit these so-called sixty-six adults into obeying you body and soul just like that creep down in Guyana and all the other madmen who have caused disaster for so many people?"

His face twitched twice, but then that little smile came back again.

"You read the papers, don't you, son?" he asked quietly. "Somebody's going to pull that trigger one of these days. Nobody's luck holds out forever, only this time the mistake's going to be a permanent one for everybody. God ain't never come out of the flames again for me since that first time, although heaven knows how many nights I burned my eyes staring into those jets looking for him again. I guess he only tells you once, just like he did for Moses and Jesus. He told the Jews once and he told the Christians once, and now he told me once. Whatever I do, I do in God's name. So you don't scare me with all your talk of cops and judges and suchlike, because they're all going to burn in hellfire before very long. And then there'll be just us, me and my flock, and we're going to start the world off again right this time. There'll be no Catholics and no Jews and no Muslims and no nothing else. Just us. God has picked you to play a part in helping this happen, so you just be a good boy and play the cards until they're all gone."

I started figuring possibilities. With my hands locked behind my back and a restraining rope on my leg, I was not about to overpower Little Orphan Annie, let alone Barrow and the hulk in the driver's seat. There was the possibility of getting to the door of the van, unhooking the catch, sliding the panel back, and leaping out on the highway, thereby catching the attention of a casual passerby, who would then alert the authorities, who would come swooping down some half-hour later to free me and put these perpetrators under arrest. Bad as my situation was, I couldn't help grinning a little as my mind piled absurdity upon absurdity.

The best bet would be to get a subtle message through to Desmond Tivy that I was being held captive and that help was needed. He was a smart man, quick on the uptake, presumably used to extraordinary situations. The least he would do would be to pass on to Dwayne Hamilton that Benny Freedman was speaking in strange tongues. Barrow would probably be monitoring on an extension phone, so the main thing would be not to say anything that would make Tivy ask straight out what the hell was going on.

Probably the best thing would be to address him as though he were the insurance agent, mention the twenty-five thousand and how it could be had only in five-thousand-dollar installments. Should I make it a month between payments? That might be too long. If they figured the end was coming sooner or it was too dangerous to continue getting the money, they might figure the five thousand was good enough and waste me straight out. Suppose it was a week between payments? That would give me four weeks' leeway, and if they had five thousand coming in every week, they wouldn't want to kill their golden goose. Something would have to happen in a month's time, either me breaking out or the force finding me. May the force prevail. Was the captain working on where I might be or was he ignoring it in hopes that I might have gone away? Moran. Was he still so wrapped up with his canaries that he didn't notice my song was missing? Or was he out there somewhere trying to sniff down my trail? If Moran got his teeth in these people, they'd know it. He could match Billy Bob pound for pound and maybe even give the Reverend Phil a run for his money.

Would they go for two weeks between payments? No, too many things could go wrong. Every week was better. Suppose I told them they could get five thousand a week for six million dollars' worth? They'd kill me right off without even waiting to see if there might be five thousand. Twenty-five thousand was good. Plausible. Those were the terms I thought in before I became a millionaire. A sergeant of police and a former bakery owner thought along the same lines.

"What was your specialty?" I asked.

"What?"

"At your bakery. What did you do best? Breads? Pastries?"

"Muffins. I used my mama's recipe for bran and corn muffins, and people would come from all over the county to buy my muffins. Each muffin would cover your hand and if you spread butter on them when they were still warm, they would soak it up like a sponge and it was as if you was biting into heaven. Haven't made muffins in quite a while."

The van took a hard right and then a left and stopped. Billy Bob slid out of the driver's seat and came back to Barrow, who handed him the rope.

"I'm going to open the door here and then the church door," said Barrow, "and you hustle him out and in the church real quick, Billy Bob."

The building seemed empty and we went straight to Barrow's office. When the door was closed and locked again, Barrow untied the rope from my leg, made a noose, and slipped it over my neck.

"Now, when you make your call," he said, "the first time you say something out of line, Billy Bob is going to pull that rope so tight that your balls are going to turn into melons. You just tell that insurance man you want your money and where to bring it."

"Where's that?" I asked.

"Where's what?"

"Where should he bring the money?"

"Ah," said Barrow, "now, that takes a little thinking. Can you get it in cash?"

"I can ask."

"Cash is what we want if we can get it. A check would add complications, and we've got enough complications as it is. You tell the man you want cash and he should bring it to . . . to . . . damn . . . can't have him bringing it to a street corner. We could have someone pick it up at his office. Hell, no. They wouldn't give five thousand in cash to somebody walking in off the street. I guess we've got to take the chance, Billy Bob. You have him bring it here to the church tomorrow evening at six. Tell him to drive around back and come in the door the way we did, and we'll have Billy Bob or Phil or both of them meet him and bring him in here to us, and he'll give you the money, and if somebody even takes a fast breath, both of you will be sorry forever and ever, as the good book says. You got that, now?"

It sounded pretty good to me. The other thing that looked pretty good was that there was just one phone in that office, which probably was the only phone in the church. They might try to listen by my ear, but there wasn't anybody going to be on an extension. I reached in my back pocket for my wallet, which wasn't there.

"My wallet's missing," I said, "and the phone number is in it."

"Look it up in the phone book there."

"It's an unlisted number. This guy is the money man of the company, and it's an unlisted number."

Barrow reached into the pocket of his jacket, pulled out my wallet, and handed it over. I noticed that all the cash had been removed, but Tivy's card was still there. I dialed.

"Desmond Tivy here."

Both Barrow and Billy Bob were standing a foot from me, but neither was trying to hold his ear to the phone. They were watching my face and listening to what I was saying, and Billy Bob was tugging harder on the rope than he realized, or maybe he was hoping that I would say or do something that would give him the excuse to put on the big squeeze. Was he the one who had put the quietus on Troo Song Dienben in the car lot, and did they have a finger clipper handy for me? Here I was being held in a weirdo church by a great baker of muffins and an orangutang, and it made me want to lift my face toward the ceiling and howl like a banshee. It was humiliating. But then again, the little corporal had taken over a whole country and almost the world. I suppose I wanted all these things to be done by the Rockefellers or a famous movie star or something.

"Desmond Tivy here," the voice repeated in exactly the same tone as the first time.

"Uh, this is Benny Freedman."

"Yes, Mr. Freedman."

"Uh, on my wife's insurance policy, the twenty-five thousand, that I can only get in payments of five thousand at a time, I would like the first payment, the five thousand dollars."

There was a pause. Desmond Tivy was assessing the situation.

"Sergeant Freedman," he said, "are extraneous individuals involved here?"

"Somewhat."

Another pause.

"On line?"

"Not quite."

"But close."

"Very."

Another pause.

"Do you want the five thousand in a check or cash?"

"Cash."

The pleased reaction was most noticeable on Barrow's face. He was hearing what he wanted to hear. Billy Bob's hands stayed put.

"Where should this be delivered?"

"To the Church of the Holy Avenger at 1264 Mullaney Drive. Go into the parking lot at the rear and come in the back door right there."

"When?"

"Tomorrow at six P.M."

"Should police be involved?"

"Yes, but with circumspection."

"Your life is in danger?"

"Most definitely."

Barrow's hand came down on the phone and up again, and I heard only the buzzing of an open line.

"You did fine," he said. "No use palavering any more than you have to."

There was a soft knock on the door, and I twisted around so fast that I almost strangled on the rope. I could feel the burn of the rough edges on my skin. Could Tivy have had someone make a call while we were talking? Was there a police car out back? Neither Barrow nor Billy Bob seemed concerned. Too soon. A police car couldn't get there that quickly.

Barrow opened the door and a tiny middle-aged

woman was standing there. She looked at me with the rope around my neck, one handcuff dangling from my left wrist, and then gave Barrow all her attention.

"Reverend," she said, "I cleaned the men's and ladies' toilets, and the water keeps running in the toilet bowl in the ladies' room. You should get Bill Fitch to look at it."

"I'll do that, Martha," he said. "Thank you very much."

"The exercises at the camp are for the whole weekend, aren't they?" she asked. "Right through to Sunday night?"

"That's right."

"I told Rolf that's what it was. He thought we were going to come back here for church on Sunday."

"No, we're all going to spend the whole weekend at the camp, Martha. We've got a lot of things to get ready."

"I'll see you tomorrow then," she said. " 'Bye, Billy Bob."

And she closed the door like she hadn't seen a man with a noose around his neck and a handcuff dangling from his wrist. She was a true nonbeliever.

"We best be getting on back, Billy Bob," said Barrow. "We've still got some loose ends to clean up before the weekend. I want everybody to work with some live ammo this time so they know what it feels like when it dusts your ass."

They kept the rope around my neck for the return journey, and Barrow tied the end around his wrist, closed his eyes, and dozed. But he was like one of those gila monsters or whatever those lizards are called, because every two minutes or so the eyelids would go up and the blank orbs would check me out.

I was churning inside, thinking about tomorrow and the payoff at the church. They would probably stake out the church tonight. Or maybe they would wait until just before the meeting tomorrow, because they wouldn't want to arouse suspicions. The captain would probably handle it. I may not have been his favorite person, but I was a cop and that came before everything else. The one thing civilians dare not do is fuck with cops. Off limits. Verboten.

I was looking forward to having Moran encounter Phil and Billy Bob. They were too young to have been in Vietnam so there would be no mercy on that account. How about me? Was I going to make it up a little to those two for playing basketball with my head? And dear Mrs. Barrow, the preacher's wife. Maybe I should tweak her titty to see if her response was more energetic than my little peter had been.

I grunted and the eyes came open to check me out and closed again. No, I would go by the book. They'd get theirs for murdering Dienben and kidnapping his son. Poor skinny bastard. If he was alive to tell the tale. Maybe I would have a few words with the Reverend Phil in the interrogation room. I'd be as openhanded with him as he'd been with Troc. All of a sudden I felt good.

We stopped four times going into the camp while Billy Bob unlocked gates in front of us and then locked them behind us. I still hadn't seen what the entrance looked like, but there seemed to be a lot of turns and barriers.

They took off the handcuffs when we got out of the van, but kept the noose around my neck. I was figuring on what to tell Troc if he was conscious, how much hope to give him about the next day. Going to see his mama and his brother and sisters. Probably be better not to say anything. But I would sit there all night hugging my knees and thinking about what was going to happen. I shivered a little as Billy Bob drew back the bolts and then pushed me through the door before slamming it behind me.

I stood there with the rope hanging from my neck, my jaw dropped, my eyes trying to push their way out of my head. We had company. For there on the floor, cradling her son's battered head in her arms, was Mrs. Dienben, her tear-streaked face staring up at me. And lying beside her, his face all bloody, unconscious or dead, was the huge bulk of Moran, his wrists strapped together with the belt from his empty holster.

15

I dropped to both knees and slid on the smooth stone the few inches to Moran's body, bending my head to his chest and gluing my ear to the bloody shirt. There was a beat, a strong, steady beat. You could not kill Moran just by repeatedly smashing him on the head.

The softest hand in the world was placed gently on my cheek with barely enough weight to keep it from floating off, and as I listened to Moran's heart booming distantly in his huge rib cage, I thought how nice it would be to close my eyes and drift away to whatever undiscovered country didn't yet know about religion or civilization or any other of the achievements of the higher animals.

I lifted my head from Moran's chest and gazed at Mrs. Dienben, marveling that she could look so beautiful despite the tears on her face and the tears in her clothes, the canyon dust ground right into her skin. Her hand had dropped from my cheek to her son's stomach and she moved it up and down on his abdomen as though seeking to rub away his pain and suffering.

"How did you get here?" I asked, wanting to put the situation into perspective, to inject some order into the madness.

"We were searching for you."

"How did you know to come here?"

"Sergeant Moran visited to my house and asked if you had been there and also if I knew of the church which purchased the van. He said you had been interested in the church that purchased the van. I could not pull from my memory the name of the church so we went to the business and then he found the address in the book and we went there. A man inside the church said that he did not know of you but that we could possibly find what we wanted at the church camp."

"We must have passed on the road," I said. "Didn't you see us go by you on the road?"

"What?"

"Never mind. What happened next?"

"Who did this to my son?"

"A large man. A cruel man. One of the men who purchased the van from your husband."

"Would he have been the one who admitted us through the gate?"

"Possibly. Didn't you recognize his face?"

"I did not look carefully at the other two when the van was purchased. Quite often, American faces all look alike to me."

"What happened at the gate?"

"There was a woman behind the gate, and she said she could not open it and knew nothing at all about anything. Sergeant Moran threatened to arrest her, and she called on the hand radio, and in a few minutes the big man, he could have been one of the three who purchased the van, drove up in a jeep and inquired as to what we wanted. Sergeant Moran asked him about you, and the man said he knew nothing, and Sergeant Moran showed him his identification and the man said we were outside city limits, and Sergeant Moran swore an army word and said we were going to look around anyway and the man opened the gate and let us in. He took us in the jeep through two more gates and we stopped in the middle of the canyon. There was no speaking all this time. When we got out of the jeep, the man said he would take us to the reverend, and we walked up to a door in the mountain that had a round stone holding it closed. He picked up the stone and pulled the door out and as Sergeant Moran moved to the entrance, the man struck him on the forehead with the stone. Sergeant Moran fell to his knees and the man kept hitting him on the head and face with the stone. I leapt on the man's arm and he wrapped it around me and threw me against the mountain. When I came to my senses again, I was lying here, and my son there and Sergeant Moran there. I have been unable to get either one to speak. They breathe; their hearts go; but they will not open their eyes or speak."

We stared at each other, holding the look in hope that somehow between us we could engender sound or movement through our hands into their bodies.

The sound came but it was that of the bolt being pulled back, and the door opened to reveal Mrs. Barrow, her gun drawn, and Phil, with what looked like Moran's weapon tucked into his waistband. The minister's wife and assistant pastor come to call.

The lady's uniform was disheveled and you could see where her light pink lipstick had been smeared above and below the lip lines. I checked Phil's face quickly to see if there were any giveaway marks there, but it was impossible to really tell. What you could tell was the way he was staring at Mrs. Dienben, and as I looked back at her I was disturbed by the way she was looking back at him. Rage surged through me and disgust as quickly, because I was instantly aware that what I was feeling could have been as much jealousy as any of the other more legitimate reactions. I started to rise but Mrs. Barrow's gun waved me right back down to the ground.

"We need medical help," I said. "Both of these men are in precarious condition, and if either one dies, it's a murder charge against those who administered the assaults, those who were party to them, and those who did not bring aid when it was needed."

"I am a trained practical nurse," said Mrs. Barrow, "and none of these men is in a life-threatening condition. I never seen such a bunch of softies. Phil here just whupped them up a little."

"At least bring us some cloths and warm water so we can cleanse their wounds," I said. "And some food."

That request startled me. It was my stomach rather than my brain that had done the talking. When the hell had I last eaten? What the hell difference did it make if I ate or not? Just like that last meal given to a condemned man—shrimp cocktail, steak, french fries, broccoli, chocolate ice cream. How many times had I read those listings in the paper? What the hell difference did it make? You need your strength, I told myself. You need your strength so that you'll be ready when the time comes. When what time comes? Tomorrow. Maybe Little Orphan Annie was right. Tivy would tell Dwayne Hamilton and Hamilton would tell the commissioner who would tell the chief who would tell the captain who would tell Moran . . . No, Moran was with me. The captain would come himself with several of the boys in blue. Tomorrow.

Tomorrow. They would come tomorrow and we'd all be free.

The music was still ringing in my ears as I watched Mrs. Barrow walk over to Mrs. Dienben, look down at her, and then look back to Phil before looking back at Mrs. Dienben again. She got that little smile on her face but before I could move or even yell, with a quick flip she reversed the gun in her hand and cracked Mrs. Dienben on the side of her skull with the bottom of the grip. Mrs. Dienben fell over Troc's body, his face sticking out from under her left breast.

"What the hell," yelled Phil, and started to move forward.

Mrs. Barrow reversed the gun again and stuck the tip of the barrel right up the soft spot under Phil's chin. He froze.

"Gaawwed," she grated, "you still dripping from the end and already making plans for the future. Maybe you ain't going to have no future the way you going. Now let's get out of here and find out from Billy Bob what happened back in town with this boy."

Phil slowly lifted his head off the end of the pistol and backed away toward the door. Mrs. Barrow waited him out for four steps and then turned again toward us. As soon as her eyes were off him, Phil's hand sank to the gun in his waist but there wasn't any real determination in the motion. She'd taken the lead out of his pistol in both his body and his mind.

"I'll send Annie down with some cloths and water," she said to me, "and something to eat. Got to keep you going for a while."

She followed Phil out the door, and I listened to the clang and the bolt being shot. The light in the small lamp flickered twice but stayed on. I crawled over to Mrs. Dienben, pulled her back from her son, and straightened her out as comfortably as possible. She was breathing normally, but there was a big blue bruise rising where she had been clubbed. Clubbed. I looked around at my three sleeping beauties. Welcome to the clubbed.

I felt cold suddenly so I pulled my legs up and hugged my knees, rocking back and forth a bit like the old Jews in the synagogue. Did they do it to obtain warmth from God?

I reached into my shirt pocket and pulled out my little stack of index cards, which had become grimy from my sweat, and the ball-point pen.

It was suddenly very important to me that I get this down for the record.

"The Reverend Bob is a shit," I wrote.

"The Reverend Phil is a shit," I wrote.

"Mrs. Barrow is a shitess," I wrote.

I wasn't sure whether "shitess" should have two T's or not, but I let it go. I just wanted to make sure I didn't forget. I replaced the cards and the pen in the pocket and hugged my knees again. God, I felt cold. And so alone. So alone.

"Cathy," I said out loud, and there was a small echo of it in the room, an echo of the last part of her name. Cathy. Cathy. Cathy. *eeeeeeeeeeeeeeeeeeee*. I was wrong. I wasn't all cried out.

16

They trussed me the same way again in the van the next day, the only difference being that this time Phil was driving instead of Billy Bob. Mrs. Barrow had seen to that little exchange, and although her husband questioned the reason, the rest of us knew why it was done.

Annie had never shown up with the water, cloths, or food during a night that had lasted forever, and I ended up using my own spit to clean up Troc and Moran a little. Mrs. Dienben had been the first to regain consciousness, followed by her son and eventually Moran.

She crawled back to where she had been before and took Troc's head in her lap again. When he finally opened his eyes and gurgled something, the tears started running down her cheeks, but she didn't say anything and I could feel that she didn't want me to say anything. What the hell could I say to her anyway? I had told her I was going to get her son back for her and she had him right in her lap, didn't she? What more could she want?

When Moran came to, he tried right away to get to his feet, but about three seconds on his elbows was all he could manage before falling back. When he pushed his head even a little up in the air, the dizziness forced him right down again. His nose was broken and two of his teeth were cracked in half, but he acted more mortified than hurt.

"Coldcocked," he kept saying. "The son of a bitch coldcocked me."

Except with his broken teeth it came out as "thun of a bith."

Moran kept going in and out of consciousness so I couldn't really hold a conversation with him. There were things I wanted to know about what was happening on the outside, and I'm sure he was curious about what might be going on where we were. We'd exchange a few words and I'd be about to pop a big question when he'd start snoring. It wasn't really a sleep; I think maybe it had to do with concussion or a cracked skull.

When they finally came to get me, I told them I wasn't going anywhere until my people had been cleaned up, given pillows and blankets and food, and Mrs. Dienben taken to a bathroom. Troc had fouled himself during the night, and I said he had to have clean clothes as well.

Phil and Billy Bob moved toward me to turn out my lights, but Barrow stopped them in their tracks. That man knew where five thousand dollars was coming from, while the apes could not see beyond their noses. Barrow sent Billy Bob out, and he came back a little while later with Mrs. Barrow and the old man, Ben, and the old lady, Annie, and they were all carrying things. Annie took Mrs. Dienben to the toilet or latrine or whatever they had, and the rest of us fixed up Troc and Moran, with me doing most of the work.

They even brought some lukewarm tomato soup, and Mrs. Dienben spooned some into Troc while I helped Moran get his down. I showed

Moran where the pail was in the corner in case he had to go later, and I even asked Annie about bringing in some toilet paper. After all, five thousand dollars was five thousand dollars. Finally, we were on our way once Mrs. Barrow turned things around so that Phil did the driving and Billy Bob stayed at the camp.

The sun was low in the sky when we came out of the cave, and I wondered exactly what day it was. I had lost all track of day and night even though they hadn't taken my watch away. For some reason I had stopped looking at my watch, and the meals had been so infrequent that my stomach couldn't tell time anymore either. I hadn't moved my bowels since Phil had hit me in the head that first time, and I wondered if he and Mrs. Barrow had destroyed the place in my brain that made my asshole work.

They set one of those adjustable visor caps on my head to cover up the bumps and holes and scabs, but they didn't try to do anything with the stubble of beard on my face. These people were from the breed who shave only for occasions. Both Barrow and Phil were clean-shaven, but I figured that was because they were the ones who were going to get the five thousand. It was their occasion.

When I stepped out of the van, I was surprised to see about a dozen of the pickup trucks scattered over the parking lot, with knots of people standing around and chatting. They all nodded gravely at Barrow, even the children stopping their running around and standing at semiattention until they were sure that it was all right to go back to their games. Barrow had removed both the rope from my neck and the handcuffs from my wrists before we got out of the van, but Phil took hold of my arm as soon as I stepped out the door, and I could feel his grip squeezing my arm at least an inch smaller all around.

When we reached Barrow's office, they sat me down in the chair in front of Barrow's desk, and Phil was told to go back outside to wait for the man with the money. I could feel my heart starting to pound when Phil went through the door. Had the word been passed? How was it going to be handled?

Barrow spelled out how it was going to be handled from our end. At the first wrong move, Phil was going to come down hard on my bones. The person bringing the money was to suspect nothing, nothing at all, and arrangements were to be made for the next five-thousand payment.

I didn't bother making an appeal for us to be freed or for Barrow to turn himself in before any further damage was done. We were beyond that. These people had gone past the point where they could turn back. It was no use telling them they hadn't as yet murdered anybody because they had put Mr. Dienben permanently out of business and kidnapped and mutilated his son and kidnapped and beat the shit out of the rest of us. In their own minds, they were only doing God's work. Although there were no intellectuals in the bunch, they were shrewd, dirt shrewd, and they had to know that God's work right then was breaking a law a minute. However, they weren't looking down the road a year, a month, or even a day. Their only hope, their only salvation, was that the big boom would come at the right moment to put their master plan in effect, and from that point on all previous bets were off. Hitler had been a paperhanger and Barrow had been a baker, so who was to say that miracles, good or bad, couldn't happen?

Barrow sat at the desk going through his beat-up Bible and making notes on a yellow-sheet pad, getting ready for a sermon to come. I almost asked him about which passage he had read to Darlene after their little romantic event, but that could have signed my death warrant right there. Rather than take a chance on my repeating it to Mrs. Barrow, he would have had Phil cave in the rest of my head.

There was a soft knock on the door and in came Phil with the captain. I felt a glow of pride as well as relief because the captain had groomed himself the way he figured an insurance man ought to look. He was freshly shaven and had attired himself in a pinstripe suit with a very spiffy maroon tie. He walked right over to Barrow's desk with a smile on his face and said "Mr. Freedman?" while sticking out his hand to be shaken. I would have bought a policy from him right then.

Barrow stood up, smiled in return, and pointed over at me. "That right there is my friend Mr. Freedman," he said. "I am the Reverend Clive Barrow, sir, and I am pleased to make your acquaintance."

Handshakes were exchanged between the reverend and the captain, between the captain and me, and between the captain and Phil, who was somewhat surprised to be included in the festivities. A chair was brought over and the captain sank into it, his huge buttocks flattening over either end. Christ, he looked like margarine wouldn't melt in his mouth. Neither of the two thought to inquire what his name might be. I wanted to ask him whether he was wired and how many backup units were waiting out there, but it was his game from there on in and I was just one of the players.

"Now," said the captain, "I have five thousand dollars in cash here, which is somewhat irregular, but we aim to please at our company, and there are some papers that will have to be signed by Mr. Freedman."

"You wanted to tell the gentleman about the next payments, didn't you . . . ah . . . Ben," said Barrow in his best thank-you-for-coming-to-the-service voice.

"Oh yes," I said, "I would like—"

"There's no need to go into that right now," said the captain. "First things first, you know." Jesus, he was good. This was how he had earned the right to plunk his fat ass in his office chair and make everybody else miserable. From then on he could make me miserable at his convenience. I could see the move he was about to make, and I was so excited that I would have thrown up if it wouldn't have spoiled the captain's scenario. He stood up and moved back two paces and turned so that he was facing both Barrow and Phil. Then, reaching inside his jacket as though to pull out the five thousand or the papers that had to be signed, he withdrew his .38 in one smooth movement and had those two turkeys in the pen before they could gobble once.

I took a moment to enjoy the looks on their faces before jumping up from the chair and standing beside the captain.

"All right, you two," he said, "you're under arrest for various crimes that will be sorted out later. You have the right to remain silent and all that bullshit. Units One, Two, and Three, haul ass."

The captain was definitely wired.

"Move over to the wall, you two," I directed, "and stay about three feet apart. Now, turn your faces to the wall and get your hands up to the ceiling as far as they will go."

I moved over not quite behind Phil, carefully staying out of the captain's line of fire, drew back my right arm, clenched the fist, and then dropped the arm again. The strength just wasn't there.

"Get down on your knees," I said to Phil.

"What the hell—?" he started to say, when the captain cut him short.

"Do what he says, punk," he yelled, and Phil, just like the rest of us when the captain yelled, did what he was told.

I measured carefully, pulled back my right leg, and then rammed the point of the knee into Phil's kidney as hard as I could. He made a coughing sound and went down.

I bent over him and spoke in his ear. "Get up, you son of a bitch," I told him. "Get up on your knees before I kick your mouth in."

It took him a minute, and by the time he had reached his original position, we could hear the sirens blaring outside as Units One, Two, and Three pulled into the churchyard like the whole thing was part of *Hill Street Blues.*

There wasn't much time so I drew back the knee again and let him have it in the left kidney. This time he fell forward against the wall, his face flat, and the blood started pouring out of his nose. I reached up and touched my head through the hat. It felt better, much better.

We could hear crashing sounds through the door, and I opened it and yelled, *"Here!"* Three blue-suits came tearing into the room, followed by Perkins, Molly Lincoln, and a detective named Dan Evans from the day shift.

"Jesus," yelled Molly, "what's the convention in the parking lot? You all right?"

"Where's Moran?" said the captain to me. "Is Moran here?"

"They've got him at the church camp," I said. "He's hurt. And they've got Mrs. Dienben and the kid."

"What's going on?" he said as he watched the policemen cuff Barrow and Phil, who was still wobbling as they pulled him to his feet. "Who are these people? Where the hell have you been? What's going on outside?"

"Those are just parishioners," I told him. "These here are the guys who killed Dienben and kidnapped the kid. The people out there don't know from nothing. It's a long story, and I think they're all nuts, but we're going to have to go out to that camp and get Moran and the Dienbens. There's another hard case out there, and a couple of people with guns, but it shouldn't be too much trouble."

"We better call for some more people to go out there with us anyway," said the captain, "including the Swatters. I never seen anything like this."

The patrolmen herded Barrow and Phil through the door into the church hall, down the stairs, and out the back door. When we came out, the light was fading from dusk to dark, and facing us in a semicircle, elbow to elbow, were the members of the church, all sixty of them. Their pickup trucks and vans were parked behind them, loaded with food and barbecue grills and tents and sleeping bags and boxes and barrels.

We stopped just outside the door, uncertain for a moment, but then the captain stepped to the front and bellowed that these people were under arrest and that everybody should step aside and let us through to the police cars.

"Why you wanna arrest the reverend?" somebody called out.

"Suspected murder and kidnapping," said the captain. "Now, move aside or you'll all be arrested for obstructing justice."

"Reverend never murdered nobody," yelled a woman.

Molly and Evans had holstered their guns, and they reached down and pulled them out again. We instinctively moved together into our own semicircle, with Barrow and Phil in the front. I didn't have a gun and felt like I was standing stark naked in the Arctic Circle.

"Start moving slowly forward," said the captain in a low voice. "If it's necessary, I'll wing somebody in the leg and that will make a break in the line and we'll go through that. Hold your guns ready, but I'm the only one will do any shooting."

He was wrong about that. As we started to move forward, all the church people brought up the rifles and shotguns they'd been holding down by their sides and pointed them right at us. Even the kids had .22's and you could tell by the way they leveled them that rifle training was part of Sunday school.

It was an eerie feeling to be standing there in complete silence facing all those weapons at the ready to blast us to hell and gone. I was the only one in our group who knew that these people believed that. We were the devils and they were the angels, and all Barrow had to do was lift one eyebrow and we were gone. I could see some people from the neighborhood who had come out of their houses to find out what all the sirens were about, and I prayed that one of them was right now calling police or the sheriff's department to come to the aid of officers in trouble. But we were a ways out in the boonies, and it would take them time to get there. Too much time.

"My brothers and sisters," said Barrow, "the time has come. God has given me the sign. These people are here to prevent us from our destiny. Take their weapons away and free me and the Reverend Phil so that we can all go out to the camp and ready ourselves for the new coming."

They moved in so fast that we had no time to even think about a defensive plan or action. The captain had said that he was the only one going to shoot, and I don't know if we were waiting for him to make the move or if it was impossible for trained policemen to fire at men and women who had committed no crime of violence.

They wrestled away the guns, unlocked the handcuffs on Barrow and Phil, and then cuffed everybody but me because they were one pair short. The ones I had been wearing when they drove me in were still in the van with the rope that had been around my neck, but nobody bothered to go look there. Two husky guys in their twenties were each holding me by an arm, and Phil came over and stood in front of me for a moment. He cracked his lips in what I took for a smile, and I also realized it was a promise. At the first opportunity, the Reverend Phil was going to show me what purgatory was going to be like. I shivered in the semidark.

Barrow quickly gave orders on heading for camp in a convoy, and everybody bustled to get to their trucks and vans. We were thrown into the police cars, one of which led the procession, another of which was placed in the middle, and the third one at the end.

They used the flashing lights on the top of the cars but not the sirens, and when we got going, it looked like the goddamnedest official-looking group you ever saw. People might have wondered what it was, but nobody would have thought to question it.

The people from the neighborhood were still standing around on the fringes when we pulled out, and I kept listening for the sirens, but it wasn't until we were entering the first canyon gate that I heard them faintly in the distance. I was in the car with Molly and Evans, but Barrow had given the drivers orders that we weren't to talk, and the one time Molly tried to say something, the driver reached back and smacked her in the face. Evans had yelled at that, and threw himself forward, so he got one too. The two of them looked at me because I was the only one who wasn't handcuffed behind his back, but I just stared ahead. They still didn't know what they were dealing with; I did.

It was pitch black when we came through the canyon gates, the sounds of the sirens still faint in the distance. When we came to the main clearing, the trucks all pulled off to the left and disappeared around one of the cliffs while the three police cars stayed in the center. When the car lights were turned off, it was too dark to see anything, and we sat there for a minute while our drivers conferred with somebody outside.

Then we were yanked from the cars and hustled to one of the tunnels. Just before the door closed behind us we could hear the sounds of automatic weapons being fired from the direction of the entrance, short, staccato bursts from maybe three different guns. The police had arrived without any idea of what they were facing, and now some of them were probably out there dead or wounded.

It would take headquarters some time to sort things out and get a sufficient force to come in and take these loonies apart, but eventually they would get the job done. Meanwhile, Barrow would tell his people that the Day of Judgment was at hand and they must fight the forces of evil until they were conquered. The only chance Barrow had to make it through was if the Russians started World War III while our own little battle was going on, and the superpowers blasted each other into rubble. The way my luck was running, this was not outside the realm of possibility.

But more likely, a lot of people were going to die or be grievously hurt before it was ended. And more than likely I was going to be one of them. Phil would see to that personally. My chances and choices were less than terrible. Even if I offered Barrow my whole six million bucks, it was too late for him to take advantage of the offer.

One thing I had learned for sure. Money doesn't buy happiness.

17

The room they stuck us in was larger than the one I'd been held in before, and the lighting this time came from a fluorescent desk lamp that would blink every two or three seconds as though it was about to go out. Two of the patrolmen still had their handcuff keys in their pockets, and the first thing I did was unhook everybody.

"Where's Moran?" growled the captain at me while the rest of the people scurried around the walls looking for a way to bust out of there. Dan Evans and one of the patrol cops were shoving against the metal door, but the best they could accomplish was a slight creak. Molly came over and grabbed me by my jacket, pulling me close.

"I've got to pee," she said. "Right now."

I looked around for the bucket, but there wasn't any in this room.

"They had a pail in the other place I was in," I told her, "but I don't see one here. Use a corner."

She didn't say another word but just hustled over to the far end and started pulling down her pants. I turned back to face the captain, but I could hear her spraying on the rock floor. I noticed one of the patrol cops was sneaking a peek, but the captain kept his eyes glued to mine even though he had a straight shot at where she was squatting. To him she was just one of his cops doing what she had to do.

"Moran?" he asked again.

"He's probably still in the room they had me in before with Mrs. Dienben and the kid."

"Where is that?"

"I don't know. There are tunnels all through these canyons, and they've been working on this for a couple of years now."

"Who are they? What the hell is this all about?"

I started at the beginning, including the lead that Darlene had given me, and about being whacked at the church, and how Moran had followed up on my question about the van and then had been likewise whacked at the camp. The rest of the group had gathered around us while I was spelling it out, and when I finished there was this silence, like nobody knew how to take it from there.

"Are they all nuts?" the captain finally managed.

"They believe," I said. "There's probably a fine line between their kind of believing and nuts. You know those revival preachers you see on Sundays or on the independent stations during the week? Not Billy Graham. The guys who sing and tell you that they bring the word of God, that what they say is the gospel right from God's mouth, and then they come out with the goddamnedest shit you ever heard in your life, and the audience applauds and holds their hands up in the air and the looks on their faces scare the hell out of you. Barrow's one of those. And he's got sixty-six people who believe—Christ, who *know*—that the world is going to blow up and they are going to live through it and take over. He says jump, they jump. He says kill, they kill. He says die, they die. They're just like the Iranians who think they're going straight to heaven if they get wasted for the cause. Taking them out isn't going to be easy, and I don't know what's going to happen to us while it's going on."

"Before we talk any more," said the captain, "let's set up something we can do the first time that door gets opened again."

That man laid down five different plans in the next five minutes, detailing what each one of us was to do, depending on who or what came into the room, and how they might be armed. For one brief shining moment I even believed that it was going to work. But then one of the patrolmen went over and pissed in Molly's corner, and as the smell reached me, I realized that you can't expect much from people who have to foul their own nest. We might be treading urine by the time they opened that door again.

I was wrong about that. Couldn't have been more than five minutes later when the bolt was drawn back and the door pulled open. Not one of us, including the captain, went into the prearranged positions. We just stood there, not even breathing.

"Freedman," somebody called out from the tunnel itself. What with the echo, I could only make out that it was a man's voice.

"Freedman," the voice called again. Might have been Phil. My body gave an involuntary shiver.

The captain signaled for me to answer as he moved to the side of the door and motioned for one of the patrolmen to get on the other side.

"What?" I yelled back. You couldn't see out into the tunnel. There seemed to be a flicker of light out there, but it only made the darkness seem darker.

"You come on out."

"What for?"

"Goddammit. You come out now or I'll give you what-for."

"What if I don't come out?"

"Then I'm gonna toss a smoke grenade in there and close the door, and you can all smother to death. You gonna come out, boy?"

The captain grimaced and motioned me out the door. As soon as I had cleared the entrance, the door was slammed behind me and the bolt shot, and a gloved fist smashed into the side of my head, knocking off my visored cap and driving me into somebody who was holding a rifle at port arms across his body. We both went down and lay there for a moment before the rifle holder scrambled to his feet. Two hands reached down and pulled me to mine.

In the dim light of a bulb at the end of the tunnel, I could see that the caller was Phil.

"Been waitin' for you, darlin'," he said, and I'll swear there was love in the voice. What Phil was about to do to me was going to give him as much sexual gratification as anything he did with Mrs. Barrow.

"Phil," said the rifleman who had gone down with me. I could see there were two other young men with rifles on the other side of Phil. "Phil, the preacher said you wasn't to touch him but to bring him on directly. Now, you went and hit him, and that ain't right. The preacher said to leave him alone for now. Those were the orders. You do one more thing and I'm going to tell the preacher."

The hands slackened their grip and let me go. The chest in front of me tightened and then I could hear the long sigh as the air was slowly let out. It was like telling a lion that the zookeeper had decided he wasn't to eat that piece of water buffalo after all. Maybe later, but definitely not now.

Phil turned his back and started to walk away, and the three riflemen, who were all in the khaki uniforms that Mrs. Barrow and the two old coots had been wearing in camp, closed in on me and we marched after.

But we didn't go out the tunnel door into the canyon. Just before we reached there, Phil pushed on what looked like solid rock and a piece of wall lifted up and away. It was a tight fit for Phil but he wedged through, and the rest of us followed. We were in another cave, better lighted than the one we had come from, and the third soldier slid the panel down behind us. We turned right and went deeper into the mountain until we came to another door, and this one opened into a huge room that was well lighted.

It looked like something out of one of those James Bond movies where you finally stumble onto the war room of the bad guys. The reverend's group had to have cleaned out a National Guard armory somewhere at some time. Or hijacked a shipment that was supposed to go to Libya.

There were weapons and ammunition boxes stacked in orderly fashion all over that chamber. Barrow was sitting behind a metal desk smack in the middle of the room, and there were three women and two men opening boxes or checking weapons on either side of him. They were all dressed in the khaki uniforms and they all wore sidearms. The men also had grenades hooked to their belts on one side and commando knives on the other.

Barrow was adjusting the head strap of a gas mask that was lying on his desk.

"I want you to make sure that everybody has his gas mask with him and ready at all times," he was telling the woman standing beside him as we drew close. "They could come spraying that stuff with helicopters at any time, and we have to be ready to protect our breathing so we can keep on shooting. You go spread that word, Emma, and make sure that everybody gets checked off on the roster for being equipped with a mask. That's a good girl."

As Emma went off to her appointed task, Barrow looked up at the five of us standing in front of the desk.

"Well," he said, fixing his eye straight on me, "God sure moved in his mysterious ways today, didn't he? The prophecy is starting to come true, Sergeant. The die is cast. The great nations of the earth are girding their loins in preparation to smite, and the wicked will be blown to kingdom come, and we shall come into our own."

I figured it was the right time to give witness.

"Reverend," I said, "what you seem to have here is a lack of communication with the real world. You are holding prisoner several policemen and two civilians. The charges range from murder through kidnapping, assault, illegal weapons, stolen property, and a hundred and seven other indictments that I'm sure the district attorney will come up with. I don't know what happened at your outside gate after we came breezing through, but it sounded like there could be some dead and wounded that I don't know about. I also don't know who's outside that gate right now trying to get in. I know there have to be police and pretty soon there will be National Guard and Army and Marines and Air Force and whatever the hell else it takes to break in and subdue you people. You've got a lot of weapons here and you seem to know how to use them, but you cannot prevail against the whole of the United States. If you try, you will all die. No ands, ifs, or buts; you will die. I know I've been saying this ever since you people hit me on the head for the first time, but you've got to give yourselves up. Some will go to jail and some will go free, but nobody else will die. And when you die, you don't go to heaven or hell or any other place; you just die. I don't know about you, but I don't want to die. I've got six million reasons to live."

That last statement caught me by surprise and I stopped my talking jag. What with not eating and not shitting and getting hit on the head all the time, and then being part of that crazy convoy racing through the night to this primeval fortress, I was so keyed up that it was all I could do to make one word follow the other in logical order. It was more than I could handle to stop them once they started.

Barrow stood up, came around the desk, took hold of my arm, and led me behind a stack of rifle boxes. Phil started to come along, but his boss waved him back, and when he only moved a little way, he waved him back some more.

"Son," said Barrow, once he was sure nobody was able to hear us, "I understand what you're saying. Don't think for a minute that I don't realize how it looks from your end. But the wheel is turning and we have to turn with it. We are committed to our destiny as laid down by the Lord. There is no turning back. You are right. There are police out there, and some of them got hurt when they tried to break through. Now, I want you to go out there and tell them that they have to leave us alone. We won't bother anybody. We'll stay right here in our haven until the ordained time comes. We have enough food for two years, and if they will go away and leave us alone, they will have no further incidents with us. You tell them that and then come back in and let me know what they say."

"I can tell you right now what they will say. They

will say that you are out of your tree, and that I
should come back and tell you to throw down your
weapons and file out one at a time, women and
children first, with your hands over your heads.
That's what it says in the manual on sieges and
seizures, and that's the only way they know how to
do it."

"Son, we've got hostages here. They ain't going
to want anything to happen to the hostages."

"You're right. If it was the Israelis, they would
blast their way in, hostages or no, but in this
country we place top priority on the hostages. That
only means that they will not stage an all-out
assault unless it's a last resort, but it does not mean
that they are just going to pack up and go away.
Look, you're the one against the wall. You're going
to have to throw them something. I've got a gut
feeling that when any killing was done, it was Phil
who did it. Throw them Phil for Dienben. Blame it
all on him. The kidnapping, me, whatever. I'll back
you up. You're a minister with no criminal record.
A jury is going to be sympathetic to your goals and
what you did in what you thought was a good
cause. You might get probation or nothing at all.
Throw them Phil."

"Phil's my right hand. I can't betray Phil's trust in
me," said Barrow. "He's like a son, a rock. He's all
my disciples rolled into one."

"He's fucking your wife," I said.

For a moment he looked old as a grimace passed
across his face. There was no anger, no hand raised
up to strike my blasphemous mouth. But for a
moment the white hair looked a little dingy, the
smooth-shaven red face pale, the eyes glassy, the
mouth slack.

"My wife's physical needs," he said softly, "have
been beyond my powers for a few years. She went

her way and I went mine. I know what she does with Phil because Phil came to me and asked for counsel the first time she approached him. I gave my consent if not my blessing. When the bombs hit and we are the only people left in the world, there will be all kinds of accommodations to be made amongst the few left. There will have to be new standards and new family relationships, such as Barbara, Phil, and I have already established. I cannot sacrifice Phil's body to save my own."

"He's a killer," I said between my gritted teeth. "He's a cruel, sadistic killer."

"Phil is what he has to be to protect the church," said Barrow. "Just as I am what I have to be to protect the church and my flock within it. Now, I want you to go out and talk to those people and find out their state of mind. You know ours. Try to explain to them that there will only be more killing, and nothing will be accomplished by it. We have trained for this very situation; we have thought of everything, every possibility; and we are impregnable through our own strength and that of the Lord."

"What if I don't come back?" I asked. "What if they don't let me back?"

"If you do not come back, then one of the hostages will be sacrificed as a penance for your sin."

"That's crazy."

"That's the way it will be."

"Which one?"

"That will be decided when the time comes."

"You want me to say to them exactly what you said to me?"

"As well as you can."

"How are you going to get me out there?"

"Phil knows the way. It has all been worked out."

"Will you talk to them on the radio?"

"Set up a band. But first I want you to go out and tell them how well prepared we are, how well fortified, how determined. Then, when you come back, we can talk on the radio if necessary. But there must be no more bloodshed. They must go away and leave us alone."

"Reverend—"

"No more talk. Go, Sergeant. Phil," he called out. "You get the sergeant back to his people, now, you hear? And then bring him back to me when he returns. And make sure on your way out that the people off duty go to sleep like they're supposed to. Got to have everybody at full strength all the time, you hear? When the Lord makes his big move, forty days and forty nights of bombs, we've got to be ready. We've got to be ready when that dove of peace brings his piece of twig to this mountain. Hallelujah."

I could tell by the looks on the faces of the men and women in that cave that as long as this man was alive, whoever was waiting outside that gate would have to take the mountain apart grain of sand by grain of sand and these people apart cell by cell before it would be over.

The only alternative was for someone to kill this man, the nucleus of the beast. Someone who could get to him. And as far as I knew, there was only one person who could qualify.

Hallelujah!

18

The same group that escorted me in escorted me out again, with Phil in the lead. As soon as the door to Barrow's headquarters closed behind us, Phil knocked me to the ground with a full backhand swing that caught me on the right side of the skull and made me see stars in the dim light of the long tunnel.

I wasn't knocked out cold and I didn't fall flat on my back, so after a couple of seconds I rolled over from my rear end to my knees and pushed myself to my feet. Phil was already moving down the tunnel. The strange thing was that I wasn't really surprised by what he did. It was almost like I expected it. If you ever get out of this, I told myself, you better have a long talk with Pavlov.

Phil stopped at the door and waited for us to catch up.

"Now," he said, "the light goes out when the door opens, so you just stand there for a minute until your eyes adjust to the dark. Roger, you hold onto shithead's belt with your left hand all the while we're out there, and if he makes one wrong move, you break his fucking head with your rifle barrel."

Even in the faint light you could see how red the young man's face had become.

"You went and hit him again, and now you're using rough talk," said Roger heatedly. "You do any of them once more, and I swear I'm going to tell the reverend as soon as we get back."

It would have been funny if it hadn't been so scary. I knew damn well that if I tried anything out there, the guy would bust my head with his rifle barrel. But here he was all upset because Phil had used swear words in the church camp and had gone against the boss's orders about whacking me. Phil didn't even look at him.

As the door opened, the bulb went out. They must have had a hell of an electrician in the group to wire all the cave doors like this. They probably had all kinds of experts—plumbers, bulldozer operators, cement mixers, TV repairmen, carpenters —whatever you needed on an ark that was going to survive the rain of bombs to come. You put a bunch of college professors on a desert island and they would probably figure out a way to get by, but you do the same thing with blue-collar workers and they'd be living in luxury by the end of the week.

There was no moon and just enough rawness in the air to indicate there might be rain in the next few hours. It felt so good to breathe fresh air that I took in two lungfuls and held them until they hurt a little bit.

Phil moved right ahead and we were just able to make out his dim form against the blackness of the night as we followed, stepping gingerly on the unknown terrain. We stopped four times before we reached the outer gate, with Phil giving some password and a quiet response coming out of the darkness. I couldn't tell if the people were dug into holes or behind barricades or what out there, but you could feel their presence on the back of your neck. With what I'd seen in Barrow's bunker, they probably had rifles with infrared sniperscopes on them, and right at that moment there was a muzzle centered on my back. I shivered in the coolness.

We finally came to what I figured was the long stretch before the turn of the outer gate, and straight down the canyon I could see all kinds of automobile headlights shining at us through the mist. We pulled over to the left behind a wall of huge rocks where five shapes were standing around a field piece. Under a tarp was a dim light from a tiny bulb that was hooked around a peg stuck between the stones. The gun looked like one of those World War II antiaircraft weapons, and the tiny light reflected off the copper casings of the belt of 57 mm. shells that were strung through the barrel. One spray of shells from that baby could do quite a job on whatever cars there were lighting up the other end of the canyon.

One of the men came over to Phil as we stopped in front of the gun. He was dressed in the khaki uniform, and he looked to be a very healthy fifty years of age or so with big scarred hands and fingers with stub ends.

"About ten more cars have come up in the past fifteen minutes," he said, "which makes for about twenty-two altogether. We let them come out and pull back the two policemen that went down when they first broke through the gate, but they haven't tried to make a move since. We tried monitoring their bands on the scanner, but we're getting some kind of echo pattern and we can't quite make out what they're saying."

"You got the white cloth?" Phil asked him.

"Yeah. Emma brought it out and we attached it to a long pole. What's it for?"

"We're going to send this here boy out there to tell those people to back off and leave us alone."

"That don't make much sense. He'll just get out there and run home to mama."

"The reverend's already taken care to prevent that."

"Should of known it. That man don't miss nothing. He's got Jesus right in his brain."

The man turned to look at me more carefully, almost like he was trying to guess my weight.

"Let me tell you how it's going to be," he said, "and listen careful or else your friends might blow your brains out before you even have a chance to pray forgiveness for your sins. We're going to shine a little spotlight right out there beyond these rocks. Then we're going to wait a couple of minutes before you step out into the light holding that flag. You don't want to get out there too soon because as soon as they see that light, they're going to train all their guns on it and start squeezing their fingers on the triggers. But once they see there's nothing there, they'll relax a little, and that's when you step out. They're still going to have you in their sights, but they will think before they shoot. Then you start walking real slow toward them, waving that flag. Once you get in the middle, you can wave it as hard as you want, but you start off doing everything slow, both the walking and the waving. And when you come back, you do the same for us, only you come slow all the way. First of all, we'll want to make sure it's you that's coming back, and second we'll want to know you're coming alone. You understand all that?"

I nodded, my throat too dry to speak.

He handed me the flag and waved a hand at one of his men, who scrambled up the rock face with a portable light, turned on the switch, and then rotated it until the spot shone on the ground about four feet to the right of the rock wall.

One of the women in khaki trained a pair of huge night glasses on the headlights and scanned the area.

"Can't make out no people," she said. "The lights are too bright coming at us."

The man who had given me the flag revolved it counterclockwise in my hands until the whole white cloth was unfurled. We all stood there another minute without saying anything, and I'd probably be standing there yet if I hadn't gotten a sharp poke in my back, and I turned my head to see Phil standing there, a wolfish grin on his face. He was all set to give me another shove that would have put me right down on my face, but I moved my legs quickly to get out of his range, and suddenly I was standing in the spotlight.

"Not too fast," I heard the man say to the left of me. "Give them a minute to get their glasses on you and see who you are. Okay, move out now."

It was no problem to move slowly at first because I was momentarily expecting a bullet to come crashing into my body. It wasn't until I had gone quite a distance that I remembered about waving the flag, and I did it meticulously, slowly at first and then faster and faster as I got closer and closer to the headlights.

I couldn't make out any people because of the glare, and I must have been only a couple of hundred feet away when I heard somebody shout, "It's Freedman. It's Freedman from homicide."

All of a sudden a voice on an electric megaphone blared out: "Okay, Benny. Come on in, Benny." I must have jumped an inch in the air from the shock of it.

I ran as hard as I could into the semicircle of

lights, and by the time I got there I was puffing so hard that I couldn't talk. Several pairs of hands seemed to grab me and pull me past the lights, where all kinds of policemen in bulky flak jackets and sheriff's deputies and a few civilians were clustered. It took me a few moments to pull out a few faces I recognized, and one of them was Deputy Chief Clarence Fowler, who was standing right in front of me.

"Well, Sergeant," he said, "are you able to fill us in on what the hell is going down around here? It turns out that you've been missing for some days, and Sergeant Moran is also missing, and your captain set up some kind of operation that had to do with the two of you, and now we've got a whole bunch of officers missing. It all seems to have something to do with this Church of Something-or-other, and now we've got a man dead and another wounded, and we still don't know what we're dealing with."

Somebody handed me a pint of whiskey with the cap already off, and I took a big slug of it, shivering as the raw burn hit my throat and then dropped down to warm my belly.

"It all started with the Dienben investigation, Chief," I told him, and then started to fill him in as I had the captain in the cave. I told him what had happened at the church and what had happened since then.

"Goddammit," he broke in once, "this is what happens when the right hand doesn't know what the left is doing."

"Goddammit," he broke in a second time, "what the hell kind of church is that in there? Soon as it gets light, we're going to move in there and kick some ass, and I don't care what the governor says."

"Chief," I said, "that isn't just a church in there. That's a small army of people who are brainwashed to fight to the death. And they've got the weapons to take a hell of a lot of people along with them."

I then described the gun at the end of the canyon corridor and all the other weapons I had seen stacked in their armory.

"God damn," said the deputy chief again. "This is one of those pissers. We phoned the governor's office to get official permission for us to assist the sheriff on this over the city lines, since we had already crossed them in the hot pursuit out here, and they told us that since a church was involved, we'd better make damn sure of every step we took, and there damn well had better not be anybody else hurt. But we don't know a goddamned thing about this church. There were only a few papers in the church office, and one of them was a personal letter from the President of the United States congratulating them on their stand on school prayer, abortion, and the right to bear arms. Who are they? What are they? Why are they doing this when Chief Sullivan is in the hospital with gallstones and the sheriff is up in the mountains hunting sheep?"

"Chief," interrupted a sergeant, "there's a TV van down the road, and they want permission to come in and set up their equipment."

"Hell, no!" bellowed Fowler. "Tell them this is an unsecured area, and I don't want any television or newspaper people up here. What's the story on the SWAT team?"

"They're coming through now. Should be here in a couple of minutes."

"Okay." He turned back to me. "Sergeant, I

know you've been through a lot, but I would like you to stay and brief the SWAT leader before you go back to town."

"I have to go back in there," I told him, pointing toward the canyon.

"Hell no. You're not going back in there."

"I told them I would."

"Promises to people like that don't mean a thing."

"He's going to kill one of the hostages if I don't go back."

I could hear the breaths being drawn in around me. These were tough cops who had seen almost everything there was on the bad side of human nature, but this wasn't any hot-blooded occurrence. The man had said that somebody was going to be executed if I didn't follow his orders.

"This Reverend What's-his-name told you that?" said the chief.

"Barrow. Yeah. That's what he said."

"And you think he'll do it?"

"Oh yes, he'll do it."

"But if you go back, he's just as likely to kill you too, isn't he?"

"There's that. But there's also the chance that he won't and that you people will work something out. But the definite thing is that if I don't go back, he will definitely kill somebody. Those people are past the point of no return."

"Even so, you don't have to go back. Nobody will ever think the worse of you if you don't."

"I will, Chief. I have to go back."

"Did he give you a time limit?"

"No, he didn't think about that. But if I'm away too long, they might think something is wrong, and they'll take action to show us they're dead serious."

"Can we wire you up? . . . Can we wire this man up?" he asked the group around us.

"They're going to go over me when I get back. They'd find a wire. Besides, they want me to bring back a radio band they can talk to you on. They were having trouble picking you up on the scanner just before I came out, and they want to set up a radio band for communication."

"Can we give him a weapon?" he asked the officers around us. "Is there some kind of weapon we can put on him that they won't find? A knife, maybe?"

Nobody said anything. Then this sergeant stepped out into the light, and as the face came into view, I saw it was Jenny Foster of the vice squad.

"I've got a twenty-two palm gun I carry in my purse, Chief," she said, "and I think I can conceal it on Benny so they won't find it when they shake him down."

"Good," said the chief. "I'll feel better if I know he's going back in there with a weapon on him."

"I'll need a first-aid kit from one of the cars," said Jenny, "and then me and Benny will have to fix it up in the back of the emergency truck."

Somebody ran to get the first-aid kit, and Jenny and I climbed in the back of the truck. One of the lieutenants started to get in with us, but Jenny waved him back and pulled the doors closed with a big metallic bang. She turned on her flashlight and started feeling around for the switch to the over-head light. When she found it and we could see everything in the back of the truck, she put the first-aid box down on one of the crates.

"I've done this myself, Benny, so I know it works," she said. "It's uncomfortable, but it works."

She reached into her pocket and pulled out a

shiny little .22 that looked like a toy but which was lethal enough when used correctly.

"It's accurate up to about six inches," she said, "so you have to stick it in somebody's ear or up his nose or right against his body in a vital area. Hit him in the arm or leg and he can shrug it off. It's got five bullets and you have to pull the trigger pretty hard."

She opened the first-aid kit and took out the roll of tape, which she tore off in about eight-inch sections.

"Now, pull down your pants and bend over," she said.

I just looked at her.

"Pull down your pants and bend over," she repeated. "We're going to hide this gun in your asshole."

I looked at her again. She was maybe thirty-five years old with brassy blond hair and not bad skin. Quite often she dressed up as a hooker and went out on the street to check out the action or work an illegal entrapment on some piece of slime who couldn't be nailed any other way. She returned my look patiently, knowing that what she had requested was outside the ordinary turn of events and that I was bright enough to realize eventually the logic of what she was requesting. I unbuckled my pants and shoved them and my shorts down to the floor.

"I haven't had a shower in I don't know how many days," I said as I turned around and bent over.

"You're going to have to spread your cheeks, Benny," she said, "and it's going to feel cold when the tip goes in. But it just goes in a little way. The rest lays against the side."

It did feel cold at first, but she inserted it so carefully that it didn't hurt at all. I could feel the strips of tape going across the area, and it seemed a bit bulky at first, but even that sensation went away. She tugged a few times here and there before she was satisfied.

"You know, Benny," she said, "you've got a lot of guts to be going back in there. When you come back out, you come see me and we'll do something about the other side."

And she reached under and gave me a little squeeze on my social gun.

"There," she said, "that'll hold. And I hope it comes in handy."

She waited until I had my clothes all together again before opening the truck doors. We hopped out and I could feel the tape pull, but I didn't get any jab from the gun. There were a lot of curious faces staring at us, but nobody asked and neither of us was about to tell. I wondered who helped Jenny tape the gun when she wore it on the street.

Fowler was waiting for me at the command post. The SWAT team had arrived while we were in the truck, and I filled their lieutenant in on everything I knew about the place, which was damn little when you got right down to it. They wanted to put a bulletproof shirt on me, but I said they would just take it off when I got back and it might arouse their suspicions about something else.

The SWAT lieutenant tried to convince the chief to let his team go barreling up the canyon spread out in the cars.

"Once we get up there," he said, "we can pin them down until the rest of you guys come up, and then we'll flatten them."

The look on his face was so eager that you could

almost taste his desire. The rest of the Swatters felt the same way, you could tell. They had so few opportunities to really blast the shit out of anything. Most of the time they set up a perimeter somewhere if a guy barricaded himself in a house or there was a robbery in progress, but they almost never had a chance to use their firepower or sniper capability. These were warriors who weren't allowed to do battle, and they were so eager that it was all they could do just to stand there. They kept checking their weapons and tightening their jackets and jumping around on the balls of their feet. And I thought one of them was going to cry from disappointment when the chief refused to let go of their leash.

"As soon as it gets light and we have everybody here," said Fowler, "we'll go in and get the sergeant and everybody else out of there." He turned to me. "You tell the captain what's going on out here and tell him not to worry. And you tell those church people we'll be monitoring Band Twenty-four whenever they want to call it quits."

"Yes, sir," I said, took one long look around at those I knew and those I didn't, turned my back on them, and started the return journey, slowly, so that the people on the other end wouldn't get nervous.

"You take care, Benny," somebody called out as I was about thirty feet away. "You take care, now."

I don't know what they thought about me and what I was doing, but it was all I could do to put one foot in front of the other. I was literally scared shitless. Which, considering where I was holstering my gun, was exactly right under the circumstances.

19

The return journey was a lot tougher both physically and psychologically. It had been one thing to walk out of the trap toward the friendly lights of my own troops, and it was quite another to go back into the trap that was somewhere out there in the darkness with people waiting to kill me with or without reason.

The Reverend Phil could have a bead on me right then, lining my shadow up against the reflection of the car lights, holding his breath and slowly squeezing his finger on the trigger. Hell, he could give Barrow any excuse. He thought I had a gun on me. He thought there was somebody with me. Barrow would chide him and maybe say, "You oughtn't to have done that, Phil," but that would be as far as it would go. And Fowler and the other cops would say that they had told me not to do it, they had warned me that this very thing might happen, but that's as far as that would go, too. And who would get my six million dollars? My will left everything to Cathy; there hadn't been time or energy to change anything. Would Hamilton and that New York State banker have to go scouring up some unknown cousin somewhere to tidy up their books again?

My right foot caught in a rut, and I went down hard, scraping both knees. I rolled over on my back and I could feel the gun pressing in on me. She had said the trigger pulled hard. That would be great to have a hair trigger up my ass that could blow me to kingdom went. "The things I do for England," I told the sky, rolled over again, and climbed to my feet. I looked back to see how far I had come from the headlights, and figured I was almost there. Another four hundred feet maybe.

Consequently, when the voice spoke in my ear, my heart gave such a bump that I thought it might break.

"You stop right now," the voice said. Once I could hear again, I realized it was the older guy who had given me my instructions on the way out.

"Why did you drop out of sight there for a minute?" he asked.

It took me a second to realize what he was talking about.

"Fell in a hole," I told him. "Skinned both knees."

"They can fix those up back at camp," he said. "They've got some good salve there."

He was serious. That was what was most frightening about this whole situation. These were basically nice people. Phil was going to break my kneecaps when he had a chance, but nearly everybody else in the camp would be ready to put salve on my booboos. Who was the enemy? My father used to go on and on about the Germans being so civilized. They listened to Beethoven and read Goethe and admired fine paintings and sculpture, and then they gassed vanloads of people and stuck others in camps and starved, beat, tortured, and experimented on them until they turned into dust.

These people who were ready to put salve on my

knees were just as ready to kill as many as needed to preserve *their* Christ for the post-Holocaust era. Let us pray on my skinned knees, and let those knees remind me of what I had to do if and when the time should come that I could do something about it.

The three young men were still there to escort me back, but Phil was not. We almost got wasted twice on the return because they really didn't know where the checkpoints were. The first disaster occurred when the lead man tripped across a wire that was supposed to set off a mine but didn't because of a bad connection, and the second time it was a matter of not hearing a sentry's soft challenge. It was the sound of bolts being drawn back that stopped us cold in our tracks.

"It's me, Roger," my little buddy called out in a voice loud enough to cause an echo, and there were shushes in the darkness on all sides of us.

"You best study those sheets again, Roger," a young girl said from our left, "or you're going to get lost going to the toilet."

There was some giggling at that, but an older man's voice immediately told everybody that this was no game, and Roger had best get going on his errand, whatever it was.

We finally made it back to where Barrow was waiting, and Phil was with him.

"You check him out?" Phil asked Roger.

The boy just looked at him blankly, no comprehension of what he was talking about.

"Did you check him for weapons?" Phil repeated, coming right over to me and patting under my arms. He didn't just pat. He squeezed the flesh and pushed his fingers in as though he was taking measure of what was where so that when he got around to paying me back for those knees in his kidneys, he would remember which bone to break where, what to pound, what to rip, what to tear. We had a date, Phil and me, and he was getting revved up for it. Foreplay. He moved his hands all the way down, feeling carefully between my legs along my thighs, fingers probing both sides of my testicles, and then sliding right down to my ankles. Then he ran his hand around my back and up into my hair, which he squeezed onto my scalp. But he never put his hand on my ass. There's got to be something about guys who are straight. The one area they don't like to fool around with is another man's ass.

"Now," he said, straightening up again, "let's open the shirt and see if anybody got wired out there."

"Were you ever a cop?" I asked him, unbuttoning my filthy shirt as quickly as I could.

"Been a lot of things in my time," he muttered, running his hands all the way around to my back. But he never touched my most sacred ass, my holy, Jenny-armed ass.

"He's clean," he said, as much to himself as anybody, while I buttoned up again and tucked my shirt in where it had slipped out.

Maybe Barrow knew, but I don't think the kid or the others had any idea of what Phil had been doing. This was the ultimate in citizens' armies.

"Time for you and me to have a little talk again," Barrow said, taking my arm and leading me over to the same secluded spot. Phil didn't even try to follow this time. He sat down at Barrow's desk and started sifting through the papers on it.

"You got any news for me?" Barrow asked.

"They're out there and they're not going away," I told him.

"We will discourage them mightily if they try to come in," he said.

"Look," I told him, holding my hand out to indicate the young boys and the other people in the room, "even if you had sixty-six Phils instead of this conglomeration, you couldn't hold out against what they're going to throw at you. They're still a little disorganized, I'll admit, but at daylight they will get their act together, plus helicopters, and they will drop these mountains on your head. Your people are ordinary citizens; they're not trained for combat, no matter how many Mickey Mouse drills you have put them through. The minute the firing starts, they'll put their heads up their asses and try to roll home."

"You're wrong, son," said Barrow. "We had people like that in the church, but they're all gone now. They either didn't have the fire of Jesus in them to begin with or they weren't prepared to make the sacrifices necessary for salvation. This flock has been hardened in the fire of their faith both in their hearts and in their bodies, and they will not falter."

I looked closely into his face, searching for some sign or other, I didn't know what. One minute he was an ignorant rube, an uneducated baker who had found a way to work his own hours and boss around a small band of people. And the next he talked Scripture like Jesus had a pipeline to his heart and soul and mind, and you knew that he really believed the end of the world as we knew it was coming, and that he was ready to lead the way to a new world. He was ready to save my soul; and he was just as ready to snuff out my life. If it hadn't been for the reality of that gun stuck in my ass, I don't think I would have known which way was up.

"Anytime you're ready to talk to them out there," I told him, "they'll be monitoring Band Twenty-four."

"Oh yes," he said. "Oh yes. And anytime they are ready to talk to us, we will be monitoring Band Twenty-four also."

He took hold of my arm and tugged me back to his desk. Phil got out of the chair quick enough to show respect but slow enough to let everyone know that it wasn't by chance he had been sitting there.

"I want the sergeant put back with his people now," said Barrow, "but I may be needing him quickly in the morning."

"I'll take him back," said Phil, grabbing my arm and starting to pull me to the door.

I yanked away from him and ran the few steps to Barrow, putting both my hands on his shirt and clenching the material in my fingers.

"Two things," I yelled, as Phil came tearing over. Barrow held up his hand and Phil stopped, poised and ready but not moving.

"If he takes me back," I said, "there isn't going to be much left of me for the morning. Second, I want to go back with Moran and the boy because they were in terrible shape when I left them, and I'm not going to cooperate one damn bit if they haven't been taken care of."

"Cooperate?" hollered Phil. "What do we care if—?"

Barrow put his hand on Phil's shoulder and shut him up.

"He banged on him twice even though you told him not to, Reverend," said Roger. "And he swore."

That boy had Jesus in his heart all right. You could tell that the swearing was weighed equally with the banging on me.

"You take him back, Roger," said Barrow, "and the Reverend Phil will stay here with me. We have things to discuss."

"I don't rightly know where he goes," said Roger, lowering his head in embarrassment.

"It's the small room in Corridor C," said Barrow.

"I don't know which one is Corridor C," said Roger.

"I do, Roger," said one of the ladies who had been stacking boxes of cartridges. "I'll go with you."

So Roger and the other two young men and the lady walked me out of the room as Barrow sat down at his desk again, and Phil kept clenching and unclenching his fists. We never went outside the mountain. Twice she lifted up those fake rocks that were really doors and three times we went through real metal doors.

"You better get your sheet and study the corridors again, Roger," she said at one point. "There may come a time when you have to move fast and there will be nobody to tell you where to go."

We finally stopped in front of a door that had a bolt in it, but I wouldn't have known if that was the right door or not because nearly all the places looked alike. But when they opened it up and let me go in, I was back where I had been taken from because there was Mrs. Dienben sitting on the floor with Troc's head in her lap, and sitting against the wall was Moran, who not only stood up as I walked over to him but stayed up as well. The grip of his hand was strong, and I was so happy that I didn't even hear the door being closed and bolted again.

There were three pie tins on the floor with stains of food on them, and three metal cups as well as a pitcher of water. At least the prisoners weren't being left to just rot in the dungeon.

"How's the boy?" I asked Mrs. Dienben.

"He is sleeping now," she said softly, "real sleep. He was able to take food and he was able to make piss in the bucket, and now he is having a real sleep. He is very hurt all over, but I think he is now all right."

It was strange but she sounded about forty percent more Oriental than she had all the other times I had talked to her. Had this whole business made her regress into her Vietnamese period again? Her face was so tired but still very beautiful, and I wished I could take her in my arms and comfort her the way she was doing for her younger son.

"What's going down, Benny?" asked Moran. "Christ, I thought the fag case was the worst thing I'd ever been on, but this is even queerer."

He wasn't trying to be funny.

I filled him in on everything I knew, right from the beginning, noting how his face reflected disbelief in almost the same spots that had bothered the others. I was having to repeat the damn thing so often that all I needed was a guitar and a catchy refrain, and I could open a show in Vegas. Because of his training, Moran didn't interrupt me even once, waiting until I had given my complete input before he raised the inevitable questions.

"What the hell kind of church is this?" he wanted to know. "What the hell kind of people do this kind of thing?"

I tried to give my interpretation of the church, the people, and the situation, but even as I was explaining it, it kept raising questions in my own mind too. The only logical explanation, the only one people would understand, was that this was a California church.

"Captain's locked up with the others," he mused to himself. "We've got to hook up with them somehow."

"I have a feeling that nothing much is going to

happen for a few days while they get this thing organized out there," I said. "A few years back the police in Philadelphia got themselves hooked into a situation with a militant black church that was armed and dangerous, and they kind of blockaded them for quite a while before it became a shoot-out. This one is a lot more ticklish because it's a white church, and they are in a lot better position than a brick house in Philadelphia. They've got a goddamned mountain with a honeycomb of tunnels, and enough weapons to retake Beirut. Christ, they've even got a mine field out there. If somebody hadn't screwed up in hooking it together, there'd be little pieces of me in orbit right now over this whole hemisphere."

I could feel myself getting wound up again, so I stopped talking and took three deep breaths. That didn't work so I dropped down and did fifty push-ups. Moran stood there and looked at me patiently as if what I was doing made sense. I stood up and took a minute to get my breath back.

"How come you came tearing out here looking for me?" I asked, changing the subject for a minute.

"Well," said Moran, "you asked me about that church van that I didn't check on and when the captain asked me where you were because nobody had seen you for a while, I went to the car lot and asked Nhu."

"You what?"

"I asked about the church that the van—"

"No, you said something else. Something about new."

"Nhu. I asked Nhu."

"What's new?"

He pointed over at Mrs. Dienben. "That's Nhu." New. Troc's mother. Vietnamese.

"How do you spell that?" I asked him.

He looked at me blankly. "I don't know," he said. "I was in Vietnam all that time and I don't know."

"It is N-h-u," she said. "Nhu."

"My father must have been part Vietnamese," I told them. "He said that all the time."

They both looked at me blankly. I reached up and felt the bruises on my head. They seemed smaller. I figured out the rest of what Moran had been about to tell me, and he seemed to have lost interest in telling it, so we left it sitting there where it was. I drank some of the water from one of the cups and thought about the gulp of whiskey they had given me from somebody's illicit pint. *You don't have to go back there,* they had told me. *You don't have to go back there.*

"We're going out of here the next time somebody comes in here," I told Moran.

"Great. Great."

But then his face fell.

"I was going to make a move when they brought us in the food and water," he said, "but there were three of them and two of them kept the drop on us while the other put down the stuff. Bare hands don't work against more than one gun. We need an edge."

"I've got an edge."

"Oh boy," he said. "You've got an ace in the hole?"

"You might put it that way," I told him, and started to unbuckle my belt.

20

Moran was in a talking mood, and it was kind of interesting to listen to the things he said through his broken teeth. After a while you didn't even try to make sense out of the words; it was the melody and overtones, the *ths* and *thses*, that sang in your ear.

On top of that I was so exhausted that I kept falling asleep whether I was standing, sitting, or out flat. The problem was that I couldn't get comfortable so I would sleep for only a couple of minutes and then wake up because something hurt in my back or my leg or my head. But even while I was tossing and turning in the effort to get a little bit comfortable, I would fall asleep again. And drop the gun.

I didn't know what to do about the goddamned gun. I wanted it to be right in the palm of my hand when the critical moment came. If I had it in my waist, under my shirt, or in a pocket, there might not be time to get it out and do what had to be done before anybody could stop me. It was made to fit in the palm for just such a situation as we were in, and that was where it had to be. But every time I fell asleep I would drop it.

Moran's eyes had practically come out of his

head when I unholstered the weapon. When I told him whose it was and how she had installed it, he blushed. There we were about to die and he could still blush. I wonder what Moran would have done if he had been in my position and Jenny had offered to install it for him.

No, thank you, ma'am. I don't really possess one of those so I'll have to make do without it. Or doo-doo. I'll have to make doo-doo without it.

"What are you smiling about?" Moran asked.

"It's not a smile," I told him. "This baby's got gas."

"What?"

Suddenly I was wide-awake, all sleepiness gone.

"We've got to be ready for whatever comes through that door," I said. "There will almost certainly be more than one of them, but this gun isn't big enough to cover a group. It doesn't shoot that far or fast, and it's so small that it doesn't scare, either. If you pull it on someone, they'll look at it with more curiosity than fear. So what I have to do is shoot somebody with it, and then we have to grab whatever guns anybody is carrying, and use them to do the real damage. So you have to be ready to move on whoever is closest to you, and when my gun goes off, you have to smack and grab like a teenage mugger."

"I'll be ready," he said. "What about them?" and he pointed at Mrs. Dienben rocking her son in her arms on the floor. The boy's eyes were open, and his pupils were following us as we talked back and forth.

"I figure we have to leave them here for now," I said. "You and I are going to have to find our way somehow to the captain and shake them loose. Then we'll try to work our way back and pick up the Dienbens. If we can get our hands on some weapons, we can maybe take over one of the caves or find a spot on the outside where we can hole up until our guys break in or talk these monkeys into giving up."

"That's a lot of ifs and maybes," said Moran.

"Do you have a better plan?"

He chewed on it for a couple of minutes. "No."

"If one pops up," I told him, "you let me know, because I'm not that sure about mine either."

Moran walked over and leaned against the wall by the door so he'd be in the best position possible when the time came. The thing about him was that he would stay there no matter how long it took—minutes, hours, days. Moran would be by that door when the time came.

I tried to figure out my own best spot, but all I could come up with was straight on facing the door. The gun felt hot in my hand and I wondered if I had a fever, what with sweating and chilling and being hit on the head in between. My mouth tasted like a Libyan peasant farmer's crotch at high noon in August, my eyes were so gritty it hurt to blink, and every joint in my body needed a lube job. I felt good. I looked down at the gun in my hand, and I think I felt better than I ever had in my life. You know who I wanted to walk through that door? Mrs. Barrow. I wanted Mrs. Barrow to walk through that door so that I could stick my little gun up her ass and give her a ream job way beyond anything Phil might be doing for her. Why not Phil? Why Mrs. Barrow instead of Phil? A little shiver went through me. Because I was afraid that this little gun was not enough to handle Phil. So my subconscious had focused on the woman. But now my conscious was focusing on Phil. I looked down at my left hand. It was steady. If Phil came, so be it. So be it.

We didn't talk while we waited. There was nothing to say, and there was no room for chitchat. I wasn't sure whether Mrs. Dienben was really aware of what Moran and I were planning. She and Troc looked like one of those Vietnamese pairs you would see on the six-o'clock television news sitting by the side of the road or in a village that had just been blasted to dust. Their job was to stay alive and wait it out until one side or the other won and then go about their lives as best they could. Had her romping with me been part of that resigned acceptance or was it because of our mutual loss or was she just attracted to me as a person?

The bolt on the door was drawn back.

In came Roger with a girl dressed in khaki, her rifle slung over her shoulder and a tray in her hand containing three slices of bread, six dried-up-looking breakfast sausages, and another pitcher of water. Roger had a grease gun slung over his shoulder.

"After you eat," he said, "the reverend wants to see you again."

He took his eyes off me to watch the girl put the tray down by the Dienbens. Moran was moving up on the girl as I placed my finger on the trigger of the gun and walked the two steps to where Roger was standing. The neck was the best place to shoot him. Stick it in a soft place and pull hard on the trigger. Roger. Shoot Roger in the neck and kill him.

He banged on him twice even though you told him not to, Reverend. And he swore.

I stuck the gun in Roger's neck right under his chin, the way I had seen Mrs. Barrow do to Phil when his eyes had been licking Mrs. Dienben's—Nhu's—body.

"Roger," I said, "you make one move and I'll blow your head off."

He didn't move but it wasn't so much that he was scared as that he was surprised. Before he got over that and did something foolish, I had the gun off his shoulder and he lifted his hand instinctively so that I could slip it loose.

Moran had done the same with the girl, and I think his problem was like mine. Instead of whacking her out, he had just circled her neck with one huge hand and pulled the rifle from her with the other. For the moment, she was more concerned with not spilling the tray than with losing the rifle. The ultimate in citizens' armies.

Moran took a quick look outside the doorway into the tunnel, and gave me a look that indicated nobody was there.

"Move over against the wall," I told Roger and the girl, getting them away from the Dienbens, although I am sure it never crossed their minds to grab human barriers. These kids were accustomed to taking orders from elders, and it was going to take some kind of extraordinary event to change their line of action. Little Palestinian or Irish or Salvadoran kids would be able to waste somebody without too much training because of what they saw every day of their lives, but Americans weren't accustomed to the extremes. Television wasn't the same as actually being there.

Mrs. Dienben started feeding Troc little pieces of bread and sausage. Their experience was not from television, and you ate when there was an opportunity.

We had the pair drop their cartridge belts and

empty their pockets and then spread-eagled them against the wall, their legs back about two feet so they were way off balance. I unfolded a large sheet of paper that Roger had stuck in his back pocket. My heart quickened as I looked over the drawing; it had to be a general map of the tunnels. There was one labeled C with a little mark to indicate the door to our room, and a place on each end where I figured the fake rock lifted to get into adjoining tunnels.

"Is this a map of the mountain?" I asked him.

"I ain't gonna say nothing to you," he mumbled, and I think he was maybe just this side of tears. What do you do about the Rogers in the world? He was feeling that I had betrayed him, had played dirty. The game was supposed to be conducted by the rules set down by Reverend Barrow. Roger was a soldier of the Lord and I was a prisoner of the Lord. Lord help us. I was just as weak as he was. Moran and I knew ways to make people talk. We could have put the squeeze on the girl, and inside of two minutes either she or Roger would have been blabbing away on anything we wanted to know. We probably wouldn't even have had to do anything physical. We could have faked them into whatever we needed just by going through the motions.

But neither Moran nor I was going to squeeze Roger's balls or the girl's breasts into jelly in order to find out if this was the right map of the tunnels. And it had nothing to do with me being pretty sure that it was the right map and that Roger couldn't read it as well as I could. These were nice kids on the wrong road, and Moran and I were nice people in the right business. After a while you reach the point where you can step on the face of Darlene's pimp without having it spoil your appetite or walk out of a restaurant once in a while without bothering to ask for the check, but these are minor aberrations from a very straight-and-narrow path. Hurting those kids would have also put us on the wrong road.

"Roger," I said, "you and I are going to change clothes."

"What?"

"You get out of your pants and shirt and put mine on."

"I ain't going to do it. You can go ahead and kill me, but I ain't taking my pants off."

I whacked his head a little with the end of the grease gun. "Roger," I told him, "you can take your clothes off by yourself, or you can have me knock you out with this gun and then take your clothes off. Now, we can have people look the other way while you do it, and you can put mine on right away before they look back, but our time is short, my fuse is lit, and you've got five seconds."

It took him about three to make up his mind, and then he skivvied right out of them, shirt and pants in almost record time. At least for that mountain. I stepped back a couple of paces, put down the gun by Moran's feet, and got out of my jacket, necktie, shirt, and pants. Roger was just about my size, and the uniform felt pretty good. I didn't envy him getting into my smelly clothes, but Cathy had bought me that suit and it was damned good material. I have a feeling that it was damned better material than I had realized at the time, but I also didn't know then that my wife was a millionairess. Just as nobody in that room knew that I was a millionaire. Six times over. Over what? Over the barrel at the moment.

"Okay, you two," I said when the changeover was complete, "turn around and sit down on the floor."

The girl was one of those stone-faced blonds, not pretty, kind of chunky. If she had been twice the size all around, I might have considered her shirt for Moran, but he would have to go it with his own. What I was hoping was that if someone caught sight of me from a distance, they would think I was one of the troops. Of course, there were two sides to that coin. When our guys came crashing in, they might just shoot at anybody wearing the khaki uniform without checking too closely. But the odds made it worth the shot.

"I don't know about leaving these two with those two," said Moran. "Maybe we should take them along."

"First of all, we don't really know where we're going," I said. "And Troc is in no shape to move fast or far. They could not only be killed but they could get us wasted as well if we got into something messy. It isn't great but I think they're safer here than they would be with us.

"Listen, Roger," I said, "we're going to lock you in with the Dienbens. We're both police officers and we're holding you personally responsible for their safety and welfare. If anything happens to them, you will either go to prison or be executed. And you will be an accessory to whatever happens, miss, and suffer the same penalties. Do you understand?"

The girl nodded, but Roger just looked at me.

"The Lord is going to make you pay for going against the reverend," he said. "The day of reckoning is almost upon us, and those who sin will burn in the fires of hell. But we're not going to hurt these people, either."

The look on his face was so sincerely mixed up that I almost walked over and slapped him on the shoulder, but time was running short and maybe the reverend was growing impatient, so we had to get the hell out of there.

"We'll be back, Nhu," said Moran, walking over and giving her a pat on the shoulder. She just looked at us. Troc's eyes were closed again. Two Vietnamese huddled down by the side of the road.

I touched Moran on the arm and we walked outside, pulled the door shut, and slid the bolt. We had to get out of the tunnel before somebody came looking for Roger.

I looked back and Moran was still standing by the door.

"Come on," I hissed.

"I hate leaving them like this," he said.

"We have to. They'll be all right. We'll be back for them."

"I know, Benny, but this is kind of different."

"How the hell do you mean different?"

"Well, Nhu isn't just a woman in a case I'm working on."

"What are you talking about?"

"Well, she and I have a relationship. I know it's wrong when you're on a case, but it happened."

"What happened, for Christ's sake? We've got to get moving."

"We've been . . . we've been . . ."

I knew. I suddenly knew what the hell he was talking about. When we got to Molly Lincoln again, I'd have to tell her that there was nothing queer about Moran. The son of a bitch had been screwing Mrs. Dienben. Nhu. He'd been screwing Nhu. I was the one who had been screwing Mrs. Dienben. Or vice versa. On both of us.

I yanked him on the arm to get him going. Harder than I had to. Much harder. But I didn't look at his face to see if he'd noticed.

21

I opened the tunnel door to the outside so slowly that all time seemed to stand still, and Moran's breathing from maybe three feet behind me took on the sound of a hard Atlantic surf. My head was plastered against the side of the wall so my right eye could peek through the crack as soon as it became wide enough. The light was gray, which meant that the clouds still covered the sky but there did not seem to be any rain falling. Our chamber of commerce always boasted about our perfect year-round weather, but I think we got wet as often as any other place in the country. When it rained during the winter months, people would invariably say, "Well, at least it isn't snowing," and when it rained the rest of the year, they would come up with it being good for the farmers or a nice change or something about filling the reservoirs. One of the things I liked about Boston and New England in general was that they accepted the weather for what it was—weather. Out here it became all mixed up in psyche and image. A perfect hothouse for people like Barrow and his church.

There were maybe eight or ten of them standing in a group some twenty feet from the door. They seemed to be installing a heavy machine gun on the back of a jeep, and there were all kinds of tools and parts scattered around. They were all in khaki, with two or possibly three of them women, and the biggest one of all was Billy Bob, who was lugging the barrel of the gun up on the seat so it could be fitted to the swivel. They were going to be there for a while.

I closed the door as slowly as I opened it and there was nary a squeak.

"We've got to try the other way," I whispered to Moran. "They could be coming in here for something or other any minute."

We scurried to the other end of the tunnel, and I pulled out the map that Roger had been using and unfolded it on the ground. It was too dim to make out anything so I unhooked the flashlight from Roger's cartridge belt and clicked it on.

The thing that caught my eye because of its tiny print was at the bottom-right-hand side of the mimeographed sheet. It said "United States Navy, 1942." Had this been some kind of secret Navy base or storage area during World War II? California was loaded with them near the coastline. Most were still in service but there had to be some that were put in reserve or sold to private parties. What could be more appropriate than to sell or give one to a church? And if maybe the Reverend Phil or Billy Bob or some of the others were members of a National Guard or active reserve unit, they could have been siphoning off weapons and ammunition for years without anybody being the wiser. Hell, if the big arms contractors could charge the government $1,692 for a bolt that sold for seven cents in a hardware store, nobody was going to notice some missing guns or ammunition or even a couple of goddamned jeeps. I wouldn't have been surprised if the church had a matched pair of Pershing tanks garaged in one of these tunnels.

There was a tiny black square on the map that indicated something on the opposite wall of where we were, and inspection with the flashlight revealed a hand catch at the spot. I was about to try it when I suddenly noticed there was something on the other side of the sheet. I turned it over, and there was another map, marked "Upper Levels." I flashed the light on the ceiling and saw what looked like a catch up there. Moran could probably reach it by jumping, but that didn't seem too efficient. I moved the light along the walls and there on the end was a series of rungs going up to nowhere. Except that nowhere was where the catch was situated.

I swung up on the rungs and pulled the catch and a piece of the ceiling swung down with stairs attached just like people use to go up to their attics. I quickly switched off the flashlight, picked up the grease gun, and motioned for Moran to cover me.

There was only blackness when I poked my head over the top of the stairway, so I switched on the flashlight again and beamed it down the alley. It appeared to be a deserted tunnel.

"Come on up," I whispered to Moran, and he was quickly beside me. We pulled on the rope attached to the bottom step of the stairway and it rose and closed beside us. We quickly investigated the whole tunnel and found it to be empty, with no rooms or doorway exits to other tunnels going off the sides. The only ways out were the stairway by which we had entered and a doorway to the front of the mountain.

I pulled the door open as carefully as I had the one down below. The outside of the door was

painted the same color as the adjacent rock face
and there was a little terrace in front of the
doorway that had a two-foot wall on the end of it. I
crawled out on my stomach and inspected the wall
face across from me but could see no openings or
people. I then rolled over on my back and looked
up the side of the cliff we were on, but there were
all kinds of outjuttings and small trees and bushes
that blocked the view for more than a few feet.

I rolled back on my stomach again and edged up
to the wall, gradually rising to my knees so that I
could peek over. Moran stayed inside the doorway
because there wasn't much room on the terrace
and too much movement could have caught the
eye of somebody who could see us without us
seeing him.

The group was still working on the jeep below
us, but I was too high up to hear what they were
saying. Suddenly there was a roar of engines so
loud in my ear that I almost jumped to my feet.
Around the corner of the cliff face came a police
helicopter churning against the wind roaring
through the canyon. I could tell that the pilot was
having trouble with the controls in that narrow
area, and the machine dipped and wobbled as he
brought it down lower and lower.

A couple of shots rang out from below but the
copter kept coming. And then the guy on the
copilot side stepped out onto the brace with a bulky
object in his hand and pointed it down at the
canyon. It was a video camera and at the same time
that I identified what it was I also recognized who
was using it. That blocky figure could be nobody
else but my old partner Julio Morales taking video
pictures so the coach could use them for a game
plan. There were a couple more rifle shots, but
Morales ignored them as he panned the camera up

and down. Even if he hadn't been wearing a flak suit, if he'd been bareass up there, the bullets wouldn't have bothered Julio. He was macho, that boy, and I almost stood up and yelled at him, the old neighborhood kid's cry, "Hey, Julio, look at me. I'm over here."

But even as that was going through my mind, there was a blazing whoosh that screamed by my terrace and whacked against the fuselage of the helicopter, blowing it into a thousand glowing pieces around a black ball of fire whose heat singed my eyebrows and shoved me down into the rock so hard that I momentarily lost my breath. The bulk of the machine came crashing down not fifty feet from me, and the last thing I saw was Julio's burning body, still strapped to the cabin interior, dropping to the end of the line. Disregarding any thought of safety and security, I raised my head over the edge and looked down where the burning pieces of the helicopter were scattered, some of them smoldering on the jeep. The people, with one exception, had scattered to the sides, where I couldn't see them. But still standing there, the long barrel of the heat-seeking missile in his hand, was Billy Bob, the Reverend Billy Bob, who had just killed one of the best friends I ever had and the pilot, whom I probably also knew. The Church of the Holy Avenger. They now had murdered three cops and put another into intensive care at the hospital. This was how they were going to save the world for Jesus Christ against the Communist menace. Julio had more love for Jesus Christ in his little finger than these people had in their whole congregation, and I was still assuming that most of them were sincere in their hearts in what they were doing. A wife and two children. And what about the pilot and the cop who had been killed in the first rush? What kind of families did they have? Something had to be done. Fast. The Barrows, Phil, and Billy Bob. They were the key. If we broke them off, the door could be shut on the others. Their training wouldn't mean diddly without the puppeteers.

I crawled back inside to where Moran was crouched. He had a peculiar look on his face, and his eyes were staring out into nowhere. The stink hit me then and I looked down and there in front of Moran was a pile of vomit, and when I looked back up I could see little driblets on his chin. He was gazing right at me, but I knew he wasn't conscious that I was there. I grabbed his shoulder and squeezed and shook, and he twitched his head a little and his eyes got all watery.

"Did you see it go down?" he asked, urgency in his voice. "Did you see it?"

I nodded.

"One time," he said, "one time we were trapped, cold turkey, with a river at our back, and they said they couldn't lift us out because of the heavy fire, but one pilot tried it, one guy, and just as I thought we were going to get out of there, some slope let him have it with a missile and he blew up all over us, all over us. And even now, even now, whenever I hear a helicopter, I get so fucking scared I can't even talk. And this time when I heard it, I knew it was one of ours, and I said to myself, I said, they're coming to get us, they're coming to lift us out of here. And then some slope, some slope out there, blew him to shit, and I thought, Jesus, this time the luck's got to be gone, this time you're not going to make it. Because in Nam, there just happened to be a squadron of armored boats going by that day, and they raked the area and pulled us out of there on the river. But there's no river here, and my luck's run out and this time I'm not going to make it."

"I'm here," I told him, "and you're here and we've both got guns and we're dealing with a bunch of fucking amateurs. We're pros, Moran, you and I, we're pros. And the captain's a pro. And we're going to go find him and then we're going to take these suckers. We're the river boats, you and I, and now we've got to go find the river."

I don't know whether it was the stench or because of how scared I was, but it was all I could do to keep from adding my pile of puke to his.

We worked our way back to the stairway, dropped it, and returned to the lower cave. I slid down those stairs on my belly, hit the bottom, rolled and went into a crouch, fanning the gun over the whole area just as we had learned when we had gone through the simulated village in police school. Textbook operation. There was nobody there. It was funny but the dim light from the single bulb made this cave seem almost homey compared to the dark one above. I called for Moran to come down, and we closed up the stairway again.

We reached the room, and while Moran kept his rifle trained on the front of the cave, I slowly withdrew the bolt, stepped to the side, and pulled the door open about six inches.

"You and the girl better stand back, Roger," I called in, "because we are in no mood to fool around."

There was no answer, which didn't surprise me. Roger was probably still mad at me for not playing the game according to the rules, and the girl wouldn't say anything unless a man or an elder told her to. So I pulled the door most of the way open, jumped into the room, and rolled to the side, coming up on my feet with the gun ready to spray. Roger and the girl were gone. Mrs. Dienben and Troc were in the same positions on the floor, but the other two were missing.

"Stay out there, John," I called out, "and keep your gun ready. Roger and the girl are gone."

I moved over to Mrs. Dienben, whose head was sunk on her chest, put my hand under her chin, and lifted until her eyes were looking at me. She suddenly looked forty-five years old and then some. It was like Moran and I were Rip van Winkles who thought we had made a quick visit to the cave above, but had come back twenty years later. The features had all pinched in so that she looked like what she was, a tiny Oriental woman of middle years.

"Where are those two?" I asked, still holding her chin in my hand because I knew that if I didn't it would fall right back on her chest again.

"Woman came," she said, "woman with burns on face and hands. Let them out and they went away."

"Why didn't they take you and Troc with them?"

Her chin pushed down against my hand and I withdrew it. She looked down at her son.

"Troc dead," she said. "He took a long breath, he gave a big sigh, he coughed, and he was dead."

I looked at the boy and it was as if he were just sleeping as he had been all along, but now that she had told me, I could see the tinge of gray in the brown face. I pulled up an eyelid and the eye was blank.

She said something to me in Vietnamese. At first I thought she was talking to herself or maybe even to Troc, but she repeated it again. And it was to me. Directly to me.

"You are speaking Vietnamese," I told her. "You must speak to me in English."

"The finger," she said. "I want the finger of the big one who did this. Troc will not sleep in heaven until we have the finger."

I looked down at Troc's mutilated hand, the filthy bandage, and the gap where there should have been a knuckle and a joint and a nail.

I could understand a mother wanting an eye for an eye, a tooth for a tooth, a finger for a finger. They had killed her husband and now her son, and she wanted revenge.

"We'll get you his whole fucking body," I told her, "but now you must come with us."

"I will stay with Troc," she said.

"No, it was a mistake to leave the two of you before. I don't know if you'll be any safer with us, but at least we'll be able to do something about it. This will be over soon and then we will come back and see that Troc is properly taken care of. But now you must come with us. It is possible that you will be able to help us get the people responsible for this, maybe even Phil, the big one, the one who did this to Troc. You must come with us, and we must go immediately, for time is short."

I was talking to her almost in Pidgin English. The more Oriental she became, the more of a jerk I became. I reached up and felt my head.

"What's going down, Benny?" Moran asked from the door.

"The boy's dead," I told him, "and we've got to get out of here."

Moran came quickly into the room and over to where we were. Mrs. Dienben slipped out from under her son and began to arrange his body in a formal position, arms crossed on chest, legs straight. She bent down and kissed him on the lips and rubbed her hands along his chest, down his stomach, and right to his toes.

I took her arm and she stood up beside us, so tiny against the background of Moran.

"What do we do now?" he asked.

"We're going out of here," I told him. "We're rats in a trap in this maze. The best thing is to get outside and hide in the bushes somewhere until we can find the cave where the captain and the rest of them are, and we can try to bust them out."

We went to the front of the cave again, and I inched open the door as I had before. It seemed like a goddamned hurricane out there. It was black as pitch and the rain and wind were so loud that conversation was impossible. I had intended taking the rifle from Moran and having him and Mrs. Dienben go ahead of me, hoping that from a distance it would look like I was a guard taking them someplace. But it wasn't necessary in that storm.

"Hold hands," I screamed, taking Mrs. Dienben's in my left as I held the grease gun in the other. I pulled her forward and headed out to the left under the cliff face. On the right had to be the log buildings that had been part of the camp. There had been brush and trees to the left and that was where I was heading. I don't know how far we went before I found the first tree by bumping into it, giving my head quite a reminiscent knock. It awoke every bruise Phil and Mrs. Barrow had put there. I slung the gun over my shoulder and stuck my hand ahead of me so that I could feel my way through the trees. I don't know how long we did this, but it was quite a while, and when I finally encountered what seemed to be a huge pile of brush, I pulled Moran down beside me and the two of us pulled out enough from the bottom so that there was a hole sufficient for all of us to crawl in.

The water still came through but it didn't punish us in the face and body the way it had in the open.

We huddled together for warmth, Mrs. Dienben in the middle, and lay there while the storm howled around us. For some strange reason, I was remembering seeing Sir Laurence Olivier in *King Lear* on television when I fell asleep. I think the last thing I said to myself was: Wait till Shakespeare hears what happened to us.

22

The wind finally died down to the point where you could hear the rain dripping through the branches, and I would doze and wake and doze and wake again, thinking that it had to be light by that time, but it never came. Finally I took a chance and blinked the flashlight once over my watch. It read 6:30 but we couldn't decide whether that might be A.M. or P.M.

Mrs. Dienben lay huddled between us, the top of her head coming only to just below my shoulders and probably down around Moran's belly button. She had not stirred once since we had crawled in there, and we couldn't tell whether she slept or was awake. My bet would have been awake.

I realized lying there that I had not told her how sorry I was that she had lost her son, and I knew I never would tell her that his beating was the one that was really meant for me. My money had saved me from that. If I hadn't promised Barrow five thousand dollars, he would have let Phil work me over for knocking out the old guard. We millionaires could even transfer death. At least on a temporary basis. Let's hear it for the capitalistic system.

However, my wife had been a millionairess and she had not been able to buy off death. Cancer

can't be bought. It comes free with the territory. I
hadn't been thinking about her at all for the past
couple of days. You might say it was excusable
under the circumstances, but that wouldn't be true.
What was true was that she was no longer in the
front of my mind. The recollections were beginning to dim, blur, fade out. Darlene had known me
better than I thought. Was this true of everybody
of like circumstances, or was I one prick in a
million? I felt Mrs. Dienben's body faintly warming
my groin area. One prick in a million. If nomi-
nated, I would have to serve.

"How long should we stay here?" Moran asked
almost in my ear.

"I suppose until our guys come in and get us," I
said. "That would be the smart thing. But I don't
know if I can do that. If I don't get some kind of
action soon, I'm going to blow my mind. I think we
should go back and find the captain."

"You people are pretty conservative," said
Moran. "So if that's what you think we should do, I
know it's right."

"What people?"

"You people. The Jewish people."

My God, I thought, the rain has seeped through
the holes that Phil put in Moran's head and short-
circuited him.

"What would your people do?" I asked him.

"Us!" he snorted. "Without thinking, we would
have run back and wasted some of the sons of
bitches."

"Well, I'm only half Irish," I said, "so why don't
we walk back and waste *all* the sons of bitches?"
And I started to snake out of the covering
branches.

Moran's huge hand grabbed me by the head,
slipped down to my shoulder, and clamped on

hard. The hot pain almost felt good in the raw cold.

"What was that?" he asked.

"What was what?"

"What did you say about half Irish?"

"My mother was Irish. Callaghan with a G. First name Deirdre. And I think she was almost beautiful when she was a girl."

"Your mother was Irish?"

"I first learned to swim in an Irish womb, and I was suckled on Irish milk that was fifty percent Jameson's."

I didn't know why I was talking this way to him. Frustration maybe. Or perhaps the rain had filtered through the holes that Phil and Mrs. Barrow had put in my head. And there was always the possibility that at that point I wanted him to like me, to be my friend. I didn't want to be alone anymore.

"But your whole name is Jewish," he said.

It took me a moment to interpret that one.

"You're right," I said. "I should be Sean Freedman. But my father was the dominant one of the pair; it was definitely a one-way marriage. And so I am Benjamin Freedman."

"Half Irish," mused Moran, and he gave my shoulder another squeeze before letting it go and starting to back out himself. "Well, that explains a lot of things."

I was too tired to open that can of worms, so I bent down and gently coddled Mrs. Dienben out of our warren. The black had turned to a dark gray so I figured the watch had been telling us it was daylight rather than dark. You could just distinguish tree trunks up to maybe five feet away.

We did a 180-degree turn and felt our way forward, or at least what we thought was forward. I held the grease gun at alert in my right hand and Mrs. Dienben's tiny paw in my left, and with her left hand she pulled the mass of Moran behind us. We went slowly and fairly noiselessly in the patter of the rain and, miracle of miracles, after a proper interval of time we bumped smack into the mountain again. At least we hoped it was the same mountain.

I felt my way along the face of it until I suddenly came across metal. My hand traced the edges of what appeared to be a door, and I finally found the handle. I worried about opening it until I remembered the switches that automatically turned off the light when the cave doors were opened.

"When we get inside," I told my pair of beauties, "stay low so that when the light comes on, whoever's in there won't have standing targets."

If there were people in the tunnel when I opened the door, they would become confused by the light going out on them. Our eyes were accustomed to the dark, while theirs would not be for a few minutes. So it would be best to wait about a minute before I closed the door and made the light come on again. Everything seemed so logical to me, and I realized that some of this had to be due to my state of exhaustion, but I was so tired that I didn't care.

I pulled the door open and we crawled into the cave, which felt quite warm compared to the outside. Then, when I figured the correct interval had occurred, I pulled the door shut again, and a dim light went on almost two-thirds of the way down the tunnel. We were the only ones in there.

We moved down to the light bulb and saw a door set into the rock about four feet past where we were.

I whispered to Moran that I was going to pull

open the door and leap in to the left, and that he should follow with a jump to the right. He took Mrs. Dienben by the arm and led her to the blind side of the door, where he pushed her down on the floor.

I yanked open the door and threw myself to the left, where I rolled once and came up on my knees with my finger tight on the trigger. I heard the whoosh of Moran going by on the right and then the "oof" as his body hit the ground.

They were in there all right, and if it hadn't been for the "Shoot/Don't Shoot" training course we had been put through at the Police Academy the year before, a lot of them would have been dead or thrashing around with wounds right at that moment. I took my finger all the way off the trigger just in case I sneezed or something.

There were two teenage girls in the khaki uniforms standing on the other side of the room. One of them was carrying a baby in her arms who had obviously been squalling when we busted in. The other one was kneeling down holding the wienie of a five-year-old boy who was whizzing into one of those all-too-familiar pails.

The baby stopped crying and stared at us with those half-dollar-size eyes, but the little boy continued with his tinkle right to the end, and we all waited while the girl zipped him up and then stood up herself.

There were maybe ten other kids in the room lying on or in sleeping bags, all of them blissfully unaware of what was going on at the time. Moran was moving around the room checking for weapons and came up with a .22 rifle, which he held in the air to show me. He went outside and returned immediately with Mrs. Dienben, to whom he handed the weapon. She took it from him in a way that indicated she had held a rifle before.

"Who's in charge here?" I asked, and the look of the one who had handled the urinary need showed that it was the one holding the baby. She looked to be about nineteen years old, while the other one on close inspection seemed to be no more than fourteen or fifteen.

"Don't do anything foolish," I told the older one, "and nobody will be hurt."

"We heard about you on the radio," said the younger one.

"Shut up, Felicity," snapped the other one.

It took me a moment.

"Moran," I said, "see if you can locate that radio anywhere."

It was lying on one of the empty sleeping bags, probably the one used by the boss lady. He switched it on and we could hear a great deal of static.

"Phil," suddenly squawked a voice from the radio, "they're moving some heavy machinery out there."

There were some more squawks.

"Are they tanks?" asked a voice, which had to be Phil, but you couldn't really tell with all the static. "Can you tell if they're tanks?"

"We can't tell nothing in this fog."

"Did you get those last mines in?"

"They're all in."

"Then just sit tight. Remember, we switch to the new band at eight hundred hours. You got your list of the bands and the changes?"

"We got it. We're all doing fine here."

"That's good. Reverend wants to say something."

In spite of the squawks, squeals, and static, I

would have known right off whose voice the next one was. If there was a God, he'd given Barrow a gift when it came to voices.

"I want you to know," the voice began, "that I am speaking to you from my knees in the middle of our mountain, and that I am praying to the Lord God to be with us on this day. For this is going to be the day that will be written in the new book of Jesus Christ and us, his apostles of the lyin, who are fighting the forces of evil so that his word will remain when all else goes. This is going to be a day of days for us, my children, the day when we meet Beelzebub on his own terms and blow him away into limbo forever. This is going to be a trying day, perhaps the last day for some of us. But remember, we have nothing to lose if we lose our lives because Jesus will take us up in his hands to sit at his feet and wait for the rest to enter Paradise. Do not be afraid of men or bullets or tanks or bombs because Jesus is on our side and we cannot lose, no matter what we lose. Let us pray."

The two girls sank to their knees, the older one still holding the baby, closed their eyes, and moved their lips in silent prayer. You couldn't help but feel a little foolish standing there holding a grease gun while young girls prayed and little children slept the sleep of the innocent. It might be necessary to kill their parents or their older brothers and sisters that day; it might even be that some of them would die in the crossfire. What was it Cathy had said to me one night when the pain was so bad that it cut right through all the morphine and made the sweat break out in big globs on her face?

"Who's in charge of all this?" she had asked. "Who's in charge?"

Me, I said to myself, *I'm the senior sergeant in charge.*

"Moran," I said, "can I see you over here by the wall for a minute?"

I moved back to the wall by the door and he followed, munching on a piece of bread he had picked up somewhere in the room. Mrs. Dienben stayed where she was, holding the rifle in the crook of her arm, eyes focused on the two girls. The older one had placed the baby down on a sleeping bag and had then sat down cross-legged beside her. Felicity had taken the little boy back to his sleeping bag and tucked him in. She was standing uncertainly beside him, not sure what she should do. I waved with the gun for her to sit down, and she immediately dropped beside the little boy, who was already asleep again.

"We've got some choices to make," I told Moran. "It's now seven-forty-five, which means that in fifteen minutes they are going to change their radio band, and we'll have trouble finding it unless these girls have a sheet somewhere with the schedule. That big one isn't going to give us anything, and I don't think we could beat it out of her even if we wanted to try. We could probably trick the young one into giving it away, but that might take time. The question is whether we want to communicate with Barrow, tell him we have our group of hostages here, and see if we can trade off for the captain and the rest of them. The problem as I see it is that these people are fanatic enough to put their trust in God and come down here and wipe us out—and too bad if some of the kids are lost along the way. Right now they don't know where the hell we are and what we might be up to. I think we should take the older one with us, because she wouldn't think twice about leaving the kids and racing off to tell about us. I think if we leave just the younger one here, she will stick with the kids and wait for somebody to come along."

"I keep expecting somebody to come along any minute," said Moran.

"I know the feeling," I told him, "but they have personnel and logistics problems. They have maybe sixty-five or seventy adults in the church. I don't think they count children and I don't know what age they consider adult. It could be that they have fifteen or twenty teenagers who are not considered members but who are big enough to blow you to hell with a gun. Even so, this is pretty big territory to cover, and they've got to have a lot of people down by the canyon entrance to stop any rush our people put on. And according to the map Roger had, there are maybe seventy or eighty tunnels in this rabbit warren. They've also got to have guards scattered around the compound. So what we've got here is like one of those bedroom comedies where people keep going through doors and missing each other by seconds. Then, all of a sudden, somebody misses a beat and you're standing eyeball to eyeball."

I was spelling it all out as much for myself as for Moran, hoping to come up with something brilliant along the way, but there was nothing, nothing, and I could feel the rage building in me as I talked. I looked over at the older girl sitting on the blanket, her face locked in that strained position just off center that goes with people whose minds are no longer capable of dealing with rational argument. You could call them true believers or you could call them dummies. Whatever, they were beyond our reach.

She would sacrifice everyone in that room, including herself, if she thought that was what Barrow wanted. I could not appeal to her on the basis of law or the welfare of the children who were under her charge. And I wanted to run over and belt her one in the face, which would have been what Phil would have done. Even as I was thinking that, I felt the tension ease out of me. Nothing, no matter what, was going to turn me into a Phil.

"Jesus," I said to Moran, "these people for whatever crazy reason murder a car dealer, and all of a sudden we're in the middle of World War III. What we have to do is—"

"They didn't kill Dienben," said Moran.

"What?"

"They had nothing to do with that."

"They were there that night," I said. "Phil practically—"

"They didn't have nothing to do with that."

"But they kidnapped Troc—"

"They got the idea from what happened before. They were only after money."

"Then who killed the father?"

"Troc killed his father."

"How do you know that?"

"He told me. He told me in the cave. He was sure that what had happened to him was punishment for killing his father. He thought he was going to die the same way."

"But why did he do it? Why would he do it?"

Moran jerked his thumb toward the rear where Mrs. Dienben was standing. "It had something to do with her. He didn't tell me about that."

"He killed his father and cut off his finger? Why would he cut off his finger?"

"He didn't tell me about any of that. He passed out for a while right after he told me, and we never got around to it again."

"But she's got to know something about it. Did you ask her why—?"

"Jesus, Benny," said Moran, "a few things have been happening around here. Our asses have been on the line ever since. We ever get out of here, we can maybe find out what went down."

I started to turn toward where she was standing, not knowing what I was going to say to her, when the door was yanked open and Roger came running in.

"Marianne," he was yelling, "they want . . ."

He came to a dead stop as he saw us, and we stood, Roger there and me and Moran here, maybe five feet apart. Here we'd known that anybody could bust in on us at any moment and were supposedly all tuned for it, two trained professionals, and Roger froze us. His gun was strapped over his shoulder, and the kid, the one for whom I had felt the mixture of sorrow and contempt, reacted faster than me and Moran on any of our best days. In the classic motion, he whipped the gun around into firing position and I could see his hand tightening on the trigger as I was still in the process of bringing my own gun up to level, and I knew that I was dead and maybe Moran too, when a shot went off and Roger's eyes almost bugged out of his head as his arms went up in the air and he crashed down on the ground. A dark spot was widening on his back where the bullet had gone in, and behind him was Mrs. Dienben, still in the alert position, working the magazine to get another bullet into the chamber.

23

The kids all woke screaming and then settled into a steady wail. Felicity came tearing up to Roger and fell down beside him, crying as hard as any of the kids. A quick glance showed that Marianne was still sitting where I had told her to sit. Her face was unreadable.

I handed my gun to Moran and knelt by Roger. He was alive but that was all I could tell. I slid my hand under him but it all felt smooth. The bullet was still somewhere inside. His face had taken a hell of a bang when he went down flat and there was some blood on him, but he did not seem to be dying. You can never know what's really going on if you're not in the business. One time I had worked an hour on a guy before the doctor finally got there, and he told me right off to quit.

"He's dead," the doctor said.

"How long?" I asked him.

"About an hour," he told me.

It was like when the doctor told me that Cathy was going to die.

"How long?" I asked.

"Four months," he said.

There she was walking and talking and still eating and able to make jokes, and the doctor told me she was dead. I wondered if there had been somebody right there in the cave with us who could have given me an answer, and I had asked how long—how long for me and Moran and Mrs. Dienben—what that answer might have been. Did I want to know? Cathy had made out a will and left all her money to me. Maybe that's what I should do. Make out a will and leave everything to the Foundation for the Cure of Dupuytren's Contractures. Six million bucks. Minus the eighteen thousand for Doc and the five thousand that the captain had brought. But then again, the fund was earning interest every day, wasn't it? Okay, six million give or take a few thousand. That would cure a lot of twisted fingers. I could have Moran and Mrs. Dienben witness it, and they would find it in my pocket when they finally trampled this bunch. That would be great for Moran to find out that I had six million dollars. He was still having trouble with my being half Irish.

"You Jews," he would say, shaking his head admiringly.

Was Roger alive or dead? I was pretty sure he was alive all right, but there wasn't a damn thing we could do to make him any aliver. He needed a doctor, a surgeon, a hospital. Quick!

I looked at my watch. Five past eight. They were already on the new radio band. But if we called them for help, they would come and wipe us out while they were getting Roger. That would be stupid on our part.

I stood up and turned toward Marianne. "Do you have the sheet with the time schedule for the radio bands on it?"

She didn't answer or change her expression.

"I want to call the reverend and tell him about Roger so they can come and help him," I said.

Nothing.

Felicity stood up. "It's in her Bible," she said. "The paper's in her Bible."

"No it ain't," said Marianne, and I'll swear she had a little smile on her face. "I ate it."

We had no time for that to come around again. Stupid girl. Then I realized. Stupid me. I took the radio from Moran and switched to Channel 24, pressed the on button, and spoke through the static.

"Freedman to Fowler," I said. "Freedman to Fowler."

I let go the button and he came in clear as a bell. "Fowler to Freedman," he said. "I read you."

"We are in a cave with a bunch of children," I said, "and we have a wounded church member named Roger who needs instant medical help. I don't know what band the church is using for internal communication so I am sending this for them to pick up and do something about it. We are going under cover in a moment. Anything I should know?"

"They refuse to give up. We have given them a deadline. We are bringing up heavy equipment. Are you free? Are you all right?"

"Positive to both. We have this radio and will contact you again. Have to go now. Out."

There wasn't any sense in taking Marianne with us because the fat was already in the grease pit, so I grabbed Moran and Mrs. Dienben and pulled them out the door. We ran to the end of the cave and there were rungs on the wall so I hopped up and pulled down a staircase. I motioned Moran to go up first and then handed Mrs. Dienben partway up until he reached down and hauled her to the top. I ran back to where the bulb was, smashed it with the barrel end of the gun, and used the flashlight to find my way back to the stairs. Just as I was pulling my foot off the top step, we heard a crash down below, a moment of silence, and then a hail of automatic-weapon fire. We pulled up the stairs and closed the hole.

"Damn," said Moran, "do you think they saw the light from up here?"

"Whether they did or not," I said, "we have to figure that they did. Let's keep moving."

There was only a side exit in this tunnel so we pulled it open carefully and I slid through to check it out first because it took Moran a relatively long time to squeeze his bulk through the narrow aperture. This tunnel was stacked with all kinds of things, boxes and crates and barrels and cartons and huge jugs of what looked like water. Some of the things were piled on each other so that you couldn't see very far. I listened carefully but couldn't hear any people, so I motioned for Mrs. Dienben and then Moran to come through. We closed the entranceway again and started to move down toward the front of the tunnel.

"I'm hungry," said Moran as we moved by cases of canned peaches. I was more thirsty than hungry, and the thought of that sweet peach juice seemed the most refreshing thing in the world. As soon as we checked out the rest of the tunnel, we should come back and get some food and drink in us to keep up our strength. Sleep was out of the question. I didn't know if I would ever be able to sleep again. Hell, Macbeth would probably sleep better than I could. Moran moved ahead of me and I dropped back to the rear, letting Mrs. Dienben pad silently by me. Mrs. Macbeth? Why had Troc said he killed his father? Had he killed his father or was he protecting someone? How far away that all seemed. The captain putting me on a hopeless case until he figured out what to do with me. Moran had ended up solving the case after all. It was he who got the confession. I wondered if he had solved the case of the four caballeros.

I was asleep on my feet, barely moving, so Moran and Mrs. Dienben were a fair distance ahead of me when a side panel opened on my right and Billy Bob lunged through. I don't know whether he was part of a crew looking for us or if he was as surprised as I was, but by the time my brain told my hands to do something, Billy Bob's huge right fist came out of nowhere and belted me on the side of the head hard enough to knock me back against an oil drum whose round edge smashed into the small of my back and rendered me numb. I never knew whether it was a nerve or something in my spinal column that was affected, but I was unable to twitch a finger as I slid down to the floor.

Billy Bob had a .45 strapped to his belt with the flap tucked in, and he reached down and pulled out the weapon, and I was looking straight into the muzzle from which my own death was about to erupt when a shot rang out and the gun fell from his hand. I don't know where that .22 bullet hit him, but it was enough to loosen his fingers for a moment. He gave a tremendous roar and whirled around. There behind him was Mrs. Dienben trying to pump another bullet into the magazine, but something was wrong, and coming back toward us at mach speed was Moran, who had dropped his own rifle for some reason and was going into Billy Bob bare-fisted.

They hit like two locomotives, the big old steam kind rather than diesel, and their fists were flying in the air and smashing into flesh and bone. Moran grabbed Billy Bob in a bear hug that brought the air out of him in a big whoosh, and I saw his tremendous right hand grasp the wrist of his left hand and both arms turn white from the pressure that was being exerted.

Billy Bob brought his right leg up in the air behind him, just as a dancer might in the process of a graceful spin, and his hand came down and pulled from his boot one of those commando knives that are more like an ice pick than a blade. I tried to push myself to my feet but there was no strength, and I opened my mouth and howled like a banshee as Billy Bob brought his arm around and jammed the knife deep into Moran's kidney. I could see the look on Moran's face as it hit, and I was gazing at death—his, mine, Mrs. Dienben's. Moran looked down at me for a moment and then I saw his hand give one tremendous pull on his wrist and heard Billy Bob's spine crack in two just like when you break a dead stick in the woods. They fell over toward me and landed maybe six inches from my feet so that I could see the knife sticking up from Moran's back, and he looked up at me and there was an expression on his face I couldn't read for a moment and then it came. There, he was saying, there, I've gone and killed somebody in the line of duty too. Then there wasn't any kind of a look anymore and the head fell down right alongside Billy Bob's.

Mrs. Dienben ran over and threw herself down beside Moran, trying to pull him over on his back, but he was too heavy for her, and she finally quit and just cradled his head the way she had her son's. Tears were running down her face and I could feel them running down mine. I was able to move my fingers again and I leaned forward and touched her. She brushed my hand away and reached over the bodies to the knife, which she tried to pull out, but it was embedded too deeply. Standing up, she yanked with both hands until it slid out, and then she sat down and hacked and sawed at Billy Bob's right hand until she had what she wanted, his right index finger. A finger for a finger. She had lost two—one by her husband, one by Troc. She still had one coming.

I was able to wiggle my toes in my boots and I bent my legs up and moved my arms, and finally I rolled over and pushed myself to my feet. The back still felt like a red-hot iron had been drawn across it, but the paralysis seemed to have been temporary.

I got down on my knees again and placed my ear over Moran's chest. There were fluids moving but no heartbeat. Billy Bob's face was enough to go on in his case. These two bulls were approximately the same size, and it was amazing that Moran could have exerted enough strength to break that huge frame in half.

Mrs. Dienben had gone down the tunnel to retrieve Moran's rifle, and was now sitting on the floor and working at whatever problem had caused her own gun to jam. This was no ordinary car dealer's wife; this was a trained guerrilla fighter back in her element. What the hell had she been through in Vietnam, this tiny little creature with the delicate features? Twice she had saved my life by pumping bullets into people's backs. There had been no hesitation on either occasion. One more second and I would have been dead. Smack on target both times. A wave of nausea passed through me, and I opened my mouth and gulped air into my lungs, faster and faster because it was as if I weren't breathing, that nothing was coming through, and I became so dizzy that I fell down on top of Moran and Billy Bob and lay there, the three of us, while Mrs. Dienben worked the magazine of the rifle back and forth, back and forth, until finally she gave a grunt of approval and looked up at me.

I pushed off the pile of flesh and stood up again. I had to have something to drink, and all I could think of were those cases of peaches back there. There could have been a platoon of people coming after Billy Bob into that cave or a bunch following the route we had taken, but I had no mind for that. I didn't even know where my grease gun was.

I walked back to where the cases were, and ripped open the carton on top. Taking a can in each hand, I went back to Mrs. Dienben and went down on my knees in front of her. It took a moment for the problem to sink in. How the hell were we going to open the cans?

I struggled to my feet again and went back among the cases, crates, and barrels, but there wasn't one damned thing there that would work to open a can. I had to have those peaches.

Mrs. Dienben had been watching me all this time from where she sat, and when I finally came back and squatted beside her, she crawled over to the two bodies and scrabbled in between them for a moment. She gave another grunt and then held her hand in the air. In it she clutched the commando knife that had killed Moran and butchered Billy Bob. She handed it to me.

I looked at it for a long moment, then pulled Billy Bob's shirt out from his pants and wiped off the blade as best I could. It took several jabs to open each can enough so that you could get peaches out as well as juice. I sat there sucking on the can and occasionally flicking my tongue into the ragged holes, feeling the edges catch and then the salt of the blood mixed in with the sweet of the sugar. Moran's blood, Billy Bob's blood, and my blood. It was going to be my church against Barrow's, and I didn't know if they drank the wine or ate the wafers, but I wasn't going to fool around with any symbols. In my church from then on we drank real blood.

It had to have been the peach juice, the rush of sugar through my system, but my head was clear as a bell and I felt strong. I picked Billy Bob's .45 off the floor and tucked it into my waist. He had two more magazines on his belt and I stuck those in my pocket. I waddled just a little with all the crap around my waist and in my pockets, but somehow it made me feel all the more secure. There's nothing like equipment to bulwark your spirit when you don't know where the hell you are or what the hell you're doing.

I wandered through the material in that cave, but it was all food or liquids or blankets or suchlike in one form or another. There were no weapons of any kind. I suppose I was looking for grenades or rockets or some kind of nuclear device. I didn't feel quite safe with just the rifles and handguns. I asked Mrs. Dienben if she wanted to keep her rifle or take Moran's, but she said that hers worked fine now and she preferred it to the other one. I couldn't fault her on that, so I took Moran's rifle and stuck it in a crevice in the wall and then bent it until the barrel was shaped like a U. I even thought about setting the place on fire before we left, but I was worried that we might have to come back in there, and that wouldn't be too nice. Sherman was working different terrain from mine.

I also wondered what to do about Moran. Should something be said over his body? We finally dragged Billy Bob away from him, and then laid Moran out on his back with his arms folded across his chest. Mrs. Dienben closed his eyes and ran her hand down his cheek, and then I closed my fist and gave his right shoulder a poke.

Then I went back and broke the bulb with the end of my grease gun and found my way back to Mrs. Dienben with the flashlight. I hadn't seen any cartons of bulbs in all the supplies in the cave. In the dark they couldn't be sure if whoever was coming was friend or foe. Me and Mrs. Dienben, we wouldn't have that problem.

I looked at the map of the caves I had taken from Roger, but I couldn't figure out which one we were in or anything else. We went out the way Billy Bob had come in, and we found ourselves in a passage that was more of a tube than a cave. You couldn't stand up in it, and on the opposite wall there were four panels you could open. We picked the one that was farthest to our right, and it opened into another tube, this one much shorter, that didn't have any light in it at all.

There was a panel at the end of this one, and I switched off the flashlight and opened it very carefully. It led out to what seemed like a short balcony. I crawled out on my hands and knees, motioning for Mrs. Dienben to stay put. The safest thing in the world for me was to have this lady covering my back.

The light was quite bright from whatever was underneath, and I stopped halfway along and carefully laid down my gun. Then I rose slowly up and slid my chin up the short wall until I could peek over the top. We were back at Barrow's headquarters. Seated at the desk was a man in khaki that I had never seen before, and a short distance away from him were a woman and a young boy, she in khaki and he in dungarees and sweatshirt, who were loading bullets into magazine holders. Nobody else seemed to be in the room. I figured it was an eight-foot drop from the balcony to the floor of the room. There was the possibility of breaking an ankle, but it could also be done without getting hurt. I motioned for Mrs. Dienben to crawl over beside me, picked up my gun, and stood up. They still didn't see me. Mrs. Dienben stood up and trained her rifle on the man.

"Everybody freeze," I called down. "This is the police and you are under arrest."

They all looked up at the first sound of my voice, and the boy and the woman did exactly what I ordered, except that they both dropped their jaws, which was a minor point. The man, after a hesitation, went for the shotgun that was lying across the desk, and Mrs. Dienben and I blasted him at the same time. My gun, of course, threw a hail of lead, and you couldn't tell how many hit him. Mrs. Dienben probably plunked him right in the middle, and this time she worked her magazine twice and put two more in him as he slumped on the floor.

I set my legs over the edge and dropped to the floor beneath me. I hit hard, but I cushioned the fall right and came straight into a standing position again. The woman and the boy hadn't moved an inch.

There was a rush of air beside me, and there was Mrs. Dienben plop on the floor from above. She didn't do as well and came up limping a bit. I motioned the boy and the woman away from where they were standing to a neutral zone, and after a moment's hesitation, they moved to where I had pointed. The woman put her arms around the boy's shoulder as if to shield him from any bullets that might be coming.

"Where's Barrow?" I asked. "And Phil?"

"They went to the front post," said the woman. "One of the bunkers caved in."

"Do you know where they're holding the policemen?"

She hesitated a moment and then she nodded.

"I want you to take us there," I told her.

"I can't do that," she said.

"Then step away from the boy," I said, "because I'm going to kill him."

Her arms tightened around him convulsively, and tears started to run down her cheeks. Her mouth moved a few times, and she gave a moan.

"I'll take you," she said. "Don't hurt my boy."

"Who's this?" I asked, indicating the man on the floor with my chin.

"That's Mr. Dunphy."

I don't know why I asked that. It was one thing to kill somebody; quite another to kill Mr. Dunphy.

"This is how we're going to do it," I told her. "I'm going to go first, and then you and the boy are to come after me, and this lady will follow you with her gun on you all the way. The first mistake you make will be the only one you'll make because she will blow you right to hell. Do you understand that?"

The lady just looked at me; the boy nodded.

"I want you to take us directly to where the policemen are being held as quickly as possible. I will keep asking you directions and you're to answer me right away. All set?"

They both nodded this time.

"Which door?" I asked.

She pointed right behind me, and I turned, walked the few steps, grabbed the handle, and looked behind me to see if everybody was lined up correctly.

Consequently, as I was turning the handle I was

looking the wrong way, and when the door burst open against me, it twisted my arm and pulled me forward and the metal banged me square on my skull. I went down in a daze as the Reverend Phil charged in and ran smack into the woman and the boy, knocking them against Mrs. Dienben, who was shoved to the side, falling on one knee. As she tried to rise and get her rifle into position, Phil picked her up and heaved her against the wall, which she hit with a soft thud with her body and a hard crack with her skull.

It took me a moment to get my arm out from under me because it was entangled with the strap of the gun, and just as I was starting to roll back to a sitting position, Phil reached down and yanked me to my feet.

I brought my knee up as hard as I could, but he twisted to the side a bit and I hit the outside of his thigh. He reached under my arms and clasped me to him, and I felt his arms go around me just as Moran's had gone around Billy Bob. In that flash of a moment I wondered if he had found the bodies and was going to make me pay in kind for the loss of his friend.

His face was close to me as the breath started to leave my body, and as my arms flailed at him, I saw that his eyes were glued on mine, and I realized that he wanted to watch me die slowly, a little bit at a time, and the thing that scared me most, even more than the knowledge that I was about to die, was that this was the way Cathy would sometimes look at me when she was still able and we were making love.

24

The thing that flashed through my mind was that my life was supposed to flash through my mind. I had read that people who almost drowned reported that they reached a certain state past the fear and the fighting where they drifted in a kind of euphoria, weightless, where the sensation was close to pleasant and relaxing. As the air was crushed from my lungs and my brain cells started to go woozy from lack of oxygen, I think I was close to that frame of mind. I could let go. Things would take care of themselves. The church people didn't have a chance of getting away from the law. Eventually, whatever force it took would break through and kill or arrest the whole bunch, and they would at a later time be brought to trial, and some, the ones like Phil, would get life or long prison terms. Most of those who had no previous criminal records would probably be put on probation and freed. Say what you want about this country, a person is still innocent until he is proven guilty. How many times had I participated in clear-cut cases where the most vicious sons of bitches imaginable had gotten off because of the lack of a piece of crucial evidence or the prosecuting attorney was an asshole who hadn't done his homework or the defense lawyer was so smart he could have reduced the charges against Hitler to littering the free world. Consequently, it didn't matter that much that Phil was killing me because they would catch up with him and make him pay. I was so tired, so tired, that the thought of death was almost a relief. When he finished me, he would put the final touch on Mrs. Dienben and then maybe he and Mrs. Barrow would knock one off before he killed some more of the people I knew, the captain and the rest of them in the cell somewhere, and maybe Jenny Foster and maybe . . . And I got so goddamned mad that I stopped flailing with my arms and jammed my right thumb square into his left eye, and pushed and pushed and pushed through the gelatinous material until I came to what felt like a piece of soft leather.

He must have screamed but I didn't hear him, and I had made and completed the move in the flash of a second so that when his arms released their grip on my back and jerked up to pull my hand away from his eye, there was no thought in his mind of doing me damage, only of stopping the pain. But my thumb had become hooked into his eye socket, and the more he tore at my hand and arm, the more my thumb and nail raked the inside of the hole. When he finally did manage to yank it out, it came with such force that I stumbled back three or four feet but did not fall down. I stood there for a moment gasping air into my lungs, air that felt of fire rather than coolness. Breathing was like trying to swallow when you have a strep throat, and I could hear my ribs creak as the air went in and out of my body.

Phil was standing there in a semicrouch with his hands covering his bloody face, howling and moaning, each beat of his heart sending pain through his whole body. I ventured two steps to see if I had the strength and the balance, measured the distance carefully, and then kicked him as hard as I could, square in the nuts. There is not a Rumanian place kicker on any team in the National Football League who could have been more on target. The pain in his eye became nothing as he fell to his knees for a long moment and then on his side.

I reached to my waist but the .45 wasn't there, nor could I see it on the floor anywhere. So I pulled the tiny gun that Jenny had given me from my pocket and put a slug in his right shoulder and a slug in his left, but I don't think he knew or maybe even felt them.

Why? Why did I do all that? The eye was to save my life, the other end of the seesaw from what I read in the novel all those years before. The kick in the groin was the other end of the seesaw from what he had done to my manhood, my ego, and my yid. The bullets in the shoulders were to neutralize those arms because inside, deep down, I was still scared shitless of Phil, not only of his incredibly powerful body but also of what he was capable of doing unhindered by pity or compassion or understanding. He was pure evil and the rest of us have trouble fighting evil because we always do it on our terms, which weakens us both physically and mentally. But every once in a while we have to stand up and fight these people so that we can live for another fifty or hundred or three hundred years on decent, human terms.

That was why the Hebrew writer laid down the law of an eye for an eye, a tooth for a tooth, a hand for a hand, a foot for a foot. That is all these people understand. The punks who rob old people and take as much pleasure from beating them up as from the few bucks they gain. The guys in the bar who laugh and cheer while a woman is being raped on a pool table. They don't pay any attention to you until you start taking their eyes and their teeth and their hands and their feet.

In this country, what we try to take is their freedom in place of all of the above. We restrict their eyes to the prison cell and yard, their teeth to the prison food, their hands to the prison jobs, and their feet to the same narrow paths every day. That's civilization.

But every once in a while on my job I have punched a punk in the eye, or knocked out his tooth, snapped a couple of fingers, or broken a kneecap. Usually at the end of a hot pursuit in a state of high, exulted fear. To the winner belong the spoils, and I have spoiled a few in my time.

But it had always been done within the guidelines of my life and my profession. That was not the case with Phil. For the first time I had dealt by my enemy's guidelines, or rather, lack of guidelines. The church people had taken something away from me, and while I was grateful to be still alive, I knew that I was never going to be the same again, and I wasn't sure how I was going to deal with what I had become.

As I stood there swaying slightly on my feet, my pulse rate began to slow down a bit and the red haze that had been cast over my eyes with every heartbeat lightened to the point where I could take in all the surroundings rather than just focus on the bulk of Phil lying on the floor.

Mrs. Dienben was stirring at the base of the wall where she had been flung, but I could not see the church woman or the boy, and I panicked for a moment as I realized I had no weapon except the little palm gun. It took me a few moments to find them huddled in the corner behind some boxes of rocket shells. The woman had her arms around the boy, covering his body with hers as much as possible. Her eyes were focused on my face as I approached, and I could tell that she was prepared to die without fighting back, and that the way her lips were moving could only be a prayer to God. It was almost a relief to know that someone in this room still had faith in something.

"I'm not going to hurt you," I said, answering her prayer. "Nor the boy either."

"We want no more of this," she said. "Whatever it really is, we want no more of it."

"I want you to go to the cave where the other policemen are," I told her, "and bring them back here."

"The boy goes with me," she said.

"The boy stays here."

"Then I don't go."

"Then I'll kill the boy."

"Then kill us both."

"Take the boy with you."

She pulled him to his feet and they went out the door behind where Phil was lying. I should have gone with them and had her lead us to the captain, but I was still having trouble just standing up, and I had no idea what kind of shape Mrs. Dienben was in. The church woman was probably heading straight for Barrow, and would return with a crew to wipe us out. Except that there had been a look in her eye. I grimaced. What you saw in people's eyes and faces reflected what was going on in your own mind. You saw what you wanted to see. The captain and the rest of them could be dead or locked up in another area. The mountain was an anthill, and I had no idea how many tunnels or passages or hideaways the Navy had constructed for whatever reason, or how Barrow had scattered his small flock to defend it. One or a dozen could come busting in at any moment. I needed a weapon.

I also needed to check out Mrs. Dienben, but when I looked over at the wall, she wasn't there, and I panicked until a slight motion caught my eye to the left. She was lying over Phil's body, her back to me, but I could see her shoulders moving, and as I came up to her, I saw that she was cutting away at Phil's right hand with a hunting knife. There was a soft grunt and she pulled her left hand in the air, holding the bloodied end of his right index finger. The count was now even. Two fingers from her family; two fingers from their "family."

She rolled off his body from the left, going over his legs and ending up on the stone floor. I waited for her to rise, but she did not move, lay there motionless while I watched the slight rise and fall from her breathing.

I walked over and bent down to pull her to her feet, but she said "No!" so sharply that I stepped back a pace.

"Something is wrong with my back," she said. "There is something broken. I can feel nothing in my legs."

She tucked the finger between her breasts and dropped the knife on the floor. What does it take to make the most incredible, bizarre acts seem ordinary? The things that happened in the German and Japanese concentration and prison camps, in the Palestinian refugee camp, in Beirut, in the war between Iran and Iraq, in the prison riots in our own country—all those seemed unbelievable when you read about them in the newspapers or even saw some of the happenings on television. As I watched her tuck that bloody finger into her bosom, right on the spot where I had licked and kissed how many days before, there was nothing in the action that seemed extraordinary to me. She was acting according to the rules of the game we had been playing; she was true to the code.

I knelt down beside her again.

"It's all over now," I said. "You have avenged your husband and your son. It's all over now."

She looked at me strangely, and I had to ask. There I was still without a formidable weapon, too goddamned weak to fight off even the boy or the woman if they came back, and I had to ask the question before I scoured the cave for a gun of some kind.

"Moran said that Troc told him he had killed your husband," I said. I wasn't able to say "killed his father." Even then, when I was being so honest that I stopped the world from interfering with my question, I couldn't say "killed his father." I had to approach it from the side—"your husband."

"Is that true?"

She looked at me for a long moment, as though she were memorizing my features for a future time when she would need to know them for a specific purpose. Cathy had always looked at me like that. And my mother. I remember once, the last week my mother was in the hospital, she had frightened me with that look, and I had yelled, "Don't look at me like that," and my father, who had been dozing in a chair by the window, jumped up and ran out of the room in a panic, not knowing where he was or what was going on. He returned about fifteen minutes later and said he'd gone for a cup of coffee. He never mentioned what had happened, and my mother and I didn't say anything. It's not a death look; it's a cling-to-life look.

"It is true," she said. Whatever she had read in

my face had been enough for her to answer my question.

"Why?"

"My husband was a cruel man. He hit me, he hit the children. Every day. Like him." Her right hand pointed in the direction of Phil.

"One day, he hit Troc very hard. Made him cry in front of his sisters. I went to Troc's room. He was lying there in his undershorts on his bed, and I held him in my arms and kissed and hugged him, and he started to cry even more and I kissed and hugged him again and told him how I loved him, and I suddenly noticed that he is hard down there, that he is sticking out of his undershorts. And I laughed and gave it a squeeze and start to stand up to go away when my husband walked in and saw, and started yelling that I was filth and Troc was filth, and he slapped us both many times and said that he would divorce me and send me back to Vietnam and that Troc would go to American jail for his whole life. That night we went to car lot, and we tried to explain what happened, and he ordered us into car and said he was going to drive to police station, and I was sitting in front seat crying and trying to tell what had happened, and Troc was in back and he found a wire on the floor and put it around his father's neck and pulled. I did not stop him. I held my hands on my husband's chest until it was over. Troc was crying that he had killed his father and the gods would punish him. So I went to the bench of the mechanic and brought back a tool and cut off the finger. Where I come from in the hills of Vietnam it was once a tradition to do this to an enemy. He is helpless without the finger of truth. And we cut the wire into little pieces and put it in the barrel, and I cleaned the tool of the mechanic and put the finger in the plastic bag we found on the bench, and we went home. We spoke long into the night about what would happen when they found we had killed my husband, but it went the way it went without our being accused. I told Troc that the gods had wanted it that way, that he had done what the gods wanted, and our cutting off the finger prevented my husband's gods from doing us harm. I had been a good daughter to my father, a good wife to my husband. I liked being an American; I liked the way I was going to live without my husband. I liked Sergeant Moran and I like you. We did what had to be done."

I didn't even try to sort out what she told me. Her voice had been getting weaker as she went along, until I had to bend my head almost to her mouth to catch the last few sentences. What she said explained Troc's fear and sense of inevitability about what was going to happen to him. I looked around the room, at the body of the guy who had been sitting at the desk, at Phil, who was now breathing laboriously, the air coming out of and into him like a small engine that needed carburetor adjustment, and at Mrs. Dienben, Nhu, her tiny body stretched out in almost two sections, as if her hips and legs had nothing to do with the upper half of her torso.

Should I place her under arrest and recite her rights to her? The right to remain silent. The right to . . . the right to . . . the right to save my life twice. The right to comfort her son. The right to protect her son. Had she told me the truth? Had she told me all the truth? Cathy hadn't told me the truth. All the truth.

I stood up and rambled the room until I found the .45 on the floor, checked the action of the gun, and stuck it back in my waist. How long should I wait to see whether the woman was going to bring back the captain and the others? What was the next thing to do? Mrs. Dienben couldn't walk; she might even be dying. Should I go looking or should I stay there with Mrs. Dienben and protect her until either the captain came or our outside group broke through? But who knew how long that would take? I found a case of grenades in the farthest corner and bent down to pull them out and string them on my cartridge belt.

I don't know whether it was because I was concentrating so hard on the grenades or she just came in that silently, but the sound of the shot going off was so startling that I almost pulled the pin out of the grenade I was holding. After that first reflex action, I was frozen for a few seconds, unable to move or think. I stayed there on my knees and carefully placed the grenade back in the box. I rotated on my knees and then raised up just enough to peek over the top of the crates in front of me. Mrs. Barrow was standing by Phil and Mrs. Dienben with her shiny revolver still pointed straight at Mrs. Dienben's head, which was gushing blood on the floor. Her back was to me so I couldn't see her face, and I moved around the boxes and came up to her as quietly as I could, which was obviously quiet enough, because she didn't stir.

The gun was still held out straight in front of her, dead on the dead target, and it could be that she was in a state of shock from committing her first murder.

I clamped one hand on her left shoulder and stuck the gun in the small of her back with the other.

"You twitch one hair and I blow your backbone

through your belly," I told her. "Now, open your fingers slowly and let the gun drop out of your hand."

I felt her whole body tense beyond the tension that had already frozen her to the spot, and then her fingers slowly loosened and the gun fell to the ground. I moved her a step to the left and kicked the gun and the knife Mrs. Dienben had used on Phil out of the way. Then I stepped back a pace.

"Turn around slowly," I told her, "and cross your arms in front of you." She did as directed and kept her eyes on the gun rather than looking at me. She trembled and shivered in alternate directions, her body seeming almost to quiver.

"Who's with you?" I asked.

She didn't answer at first, but when I raised the tip of the gun slightly, she started to babble, saying that Barrow had sent her to look for Phil, and they were expecting an attack down the canyon any minute, and everybody was dug into holes and the bunkers, and, no, they weren't monitoring Channel 24 all the time, and she didn't know anything about Roger or us being loose and she would do anything, anything, if I would just not hurt her.

"Hurt you?" I said. "I'm going to kill you. You just committed a cold-blooded murder in front of my eyes and you ask me not to hurt you?"

She started to cry as I moved closer to her, and unfolded her arms and fell on her knees, thrusting her head into my groin in the instinctive way that women like her have of going for the absolute basics without even realizing what they are doing.

I looked down at Mrs. Dienben lying there in her own crimson pool. She and her son had started the whole bloody cycle and now it had come full circle for both of them. But she had saved my life twice in the process. I owed her for that and I owed plenty on my own. I could feel the tears wetting through my pants and heard the wails and moans, the begging and the pleading from this woman who had pinched my pecker and tenderized my head to the point of a blue-plate special in a cheap cafeteria. She was a cockroach in an operating amphitheater. I placed the muzzle of the gun right on the tip of her nose, waited until her eyes became as big as quarters and the saliva dripped from both corners of her mouth, then quickly reversed the barrel and gave her a smash on the head with the butt that made me feel about as good as a man could under circumstances that were less than optimal. She toppled into the pool of blood around Mrs. Dienben, and I looked down at their two heads, one so blond, one so dark, and the tears started dripping from my eyes again, and out loud in that huge room of rock, I called out, "Cathy, Cathy, Cathy . . ." and the stone echoed me once again:

eeeeeeeeeeeeeeeeeeeeeeeeeeeeeeeeeeeeee.

25

There was plenty of rope in the room and I trussed Mrs. Barrow to the point where you could see only her feet and head. Her breathing was shallow but her pulse was strong and although the spot on her skull where the gun barrel had hit was squishy to the touch, her thick head of hair had saved her from even a cut on her scalp and there was no blood.

I dragged her into a far corner behind some crates and threw mattress covers over her. I wanted her alive for her trial but I didn't take particular care to see that she could breathe properly under the pile. I had convinced myself that the worst was over, that nothing more could possibly happen, and that any minute the bluecoats would come charging in to tell me that my shift was over and I could go home now.

However, I also was convinced at the same time that the lady and the boy had not gone for the captain, but had either skedaddled to a refuge deep in the mountain or run straight to Barrow. So much for her honest face and protestations of fealty.

"She's out of the club," I kept muttering to myself as I hung grenades from my belt and stuck magazines of bullets into the two pouches that hung from a sling I tucked over my shoulder. The .45 was too heavy and too awkward in my waist so I threw that in a box. The automatic rifle was Czech-made, according to the stamp on the metal, and they were supposed to be the best. No sense screwing around with a handgun that was little more accurate than the tiny one Jenny had given me. I contemplated Phil's shoulders again before I tossed the big gun away, but decided he wasn't going anywhere. His breathing had quieted down somewhat, but it was obvious that breathing was about all he was going to be able to do for a while. I threw some mattress covers over him, too. I tried to keep a tidy abattoir.

It suddenly occurred to me that I was in charge of enemy headquarters and there had to be something I could do to end the war. My tussle with Phil had smashed the radio, and I scoured the place looking for another one, but the only thing I found was a cheap little clock radio that was minus its batteries. By this time there had to be more media covering the event than at a Democratic convention, and it was possible that a news broadcast would have told me what the hell was going down. One time I saw a cartoon where these guys were climbing an impossible mountain a fingerhold at a time, and on the top of it on a grassy meadow a bunch of Girl Scouts were having a picnic. I could be breaking my ass inside this mountain, killing and maiming and possibly vice versa, and on the outside they could be hauling the church bunch off in paddy wagons. There were no radios or batteries for the one I had found.

I couldn't look at Mrs. Dienben. It was like when Cathy died. I kept walking around that huge room, this way and that, but I always ended up facing the other way whenever I came near her. It was time; time to face up to a lot of things.

I picked up two of the mattress covers and knelt down beside her and tried to clean her up a little. The goddamned bullet must have had one of those doctored tips because it had taken a lot of the back of her skull off. I folded one of the covers and placed it under her head, working the ends so they came up by her ears and hid the damage in back. She and her son had started the whole mess in the first place with their little bit of messing around, although I had a feeling there was a hell of a lot more to it than she had told me. That's why policemen burn out so often. They are never able to deal with situations where white is white and black is black, especially when they are dealing with people who are white and black and, like in her case, in between. There aren't always two sides to a story; there are as many sides as there are people involved.

But it could have been the way she had told it. That's always one of the possibilities. And when they did what they did, Barrow did what he did, and Phil and Mrs. Barrow did what they did—and here we were, all of us, some dead and some alive, and maybe more to be dead.

It could have been that without the murder of Dienben, Barrow and his group would have just gone on storing their nuts for the nuclear winter and training and waiting for the big bomb, and when it didn't come, the church might have just fizzled out into nothing. Barrow would have gone back to being a baker, and I might have bought his corn muffins and never known how close I came to dying from the hands that kneaded the dough or whatever the hell you did to corn-muffin batter. It could still happen, of course. The son of a bitch might be about to enter this room with his gang and blow me to hell and gone.

I gave her breast a little squeeze and stood up. I think she might have liked that.

Somehow I had to find out what was going on outside. I pulled Roger's map from my pocket and studied it. The big room I was in was the only thing that stood out from all the other passageways, and I traced how I could get out on that little balcony that Moran and I had used when Billy Bob shot down the helicopter. Where the hell was everybody? I wanted someone to come into that room even if it meant a shoot-out. At least it would give me a point from which to operate. Were Phil and Mrs. Barrow and I the only ones in the mountain? I went over the map again, hoping to find a way to where the captain and the others might be, but all those tunnels looked the same. My only choices were to go straight outside at ground level or find that balcony again and take some bearings. The balcony made more sense. Once I stepped outside on ground level, I could be duck soup. From the balcony I could reconnoiter. I liked that word. Reconnoiter. I shook my body to hear the equipment rattle, took one more look around, and headed out through the side door.

The light was out in that tunnel and I had to use the flashlight. I found the rungs at the end and pulled down the hatchway, went up slowly, and found that tunnel dark too. Either the power was going flooey or somebody was throwing switches or the bulbs were burning out because of the inconsistent voltage from the generator. Or none or all of the above.

I went through two more side tunnels and then moved forward to the outside door. I pulled it open slowly, but even then the bright light from the crack almost blinded me. The storm had passed. I knew it was the right place because I put my hand down on the pile of dried puke that Moran had tossed there. It took me a few seconds to remember what it was, and then for some reason I didn't pull my hand right away. I left it there for a short time and my eyes got all wet. He was due for a more formal memorial service than that, but he wouldn't get one any more from the heart than mine was.

I pulled the door open so that I could slither through, and worked my chin up the little wall again until I could see over the edge. At first it all looked deserted, but as my eyes rested on a spot for a while, there would be a bit of movement, and finally I made out people in holes and camouflaged bunkers and crevices in the cliffs all down the line of the canyon. You couldn't see more than an arm or a head or a little piece of the khaki uniform, but they were there all right, maybe fifteen spots that I could make out.

Then all of a sudden, standing up straight and tall, wearing the khaki like everybody else and sporting a pearl-handled revolver on his belt just like General Patton in World War II, came Barrow around the corner from where the front gate lay. He wasn't skulking around in holes or bunkers or crevices; he was marching tall.

He had a word with everybody he passed, stopping to pat somebody on the head, and once he even knelt for a couple of minutes and prayed with a girl who put down her rifle and came out of her hole to join him.

When he had come maybe half the distance from where I was, he stopped and looked around for a moment.

"Anybody seen the Reverend Phil?" he asked in a voice loud enough to be heard in both directions. The woman and the boy had not gone to Barrow obviously. Might have to let her back in the club.

Out of the silence, finally, a reedy voice called out that maybe he'd seen Phil go into the mountain sometime before. Couldn't be sure. It might have been just after the boy came around with the water for everybody.

Barrow spoke into his radio for a minute, but I couldn't even read his lips at that distance. Whatever answer came back made him turn and look at the mountain just under where I was. He had only to raise his eyes three inches to have been staring straight at me, and I nervously moved my gun closer to my body.

"I'm going in to see what the Reverend Phil is up to," he called out to those around him. "You keep your eyes peeled for anything those people might do out there. We won't have to hold them off much longer. The Lord says that this is the week it is going to happen, and then we will just hole up in our haven until we are the only ones left. But they might send another helicopter or try to come crashing through again, and we must be ready, we must fight the Devil when he appears."

I could hear the amens from all sides. They hadn't said any amens in the church at the sermon I attended. The times they were a-changing.

Barrow turned and started to walk toward the tunnel door under my balcony. Once he got in there and found the carnage in the headquarters room, he would pull in troops and go after my ass. Six of one and half-dozen of another. Maybe if I got things stirring up, the people on the outside would come tearing in. At the least, if I brought dread and confusion on those outside my door, there would be time for me to scurry back inside and get lost in the upper reaches. The reverend had to guard his outside battlefield with most of his people, and couldn't bring too many in to hunt for me. And besides, I could still feel the imprint of Moran's puke on the palm of my left hand.

I pulled the pins from two grenades and arched them in Barrow's general direction. They came down out of the blue on them so they didn't know what the hell was going on for maybe two seconds. Then someone yelled *"Grenade!"* in the kind of voice you use to yell *"Grenade!"*, and there were all kinds of shouts and yells and even a scream. But there were no goddamned explosions.

I peeked over the edge again and saw Barrow looking up from a prone position on the floor of the canyon, and lying right next to him was one of the grenades. The other one had bounced somewhere and disappeared.

Duds!

Where the hell did these people buy or steal their hardware? You could understand why the thought of my twenty-five thousand dollars had made them all drool with anticipation. I quickly ripped the pins out of the other three grenades from the belt and tossed them out too.

"He's up there," somebody yelled, just as the single explosion occurred. One of them had gone off, and I raised my head to see what had happened, and a bullet went slamming into the rock just above me.

I moved over to the left, stood up quickly, and fired a burst from the Czech gun. The sound of the richochets was even more incredible than the original shots, and just before I ducked down again I saw a young man reach out and pull Barrow into his shelter. Two of the people were standing right up in their holes looking at where I was. Not shooting, just looking.

But then everybody and his brother seemed to cut loose at the wall in front of me and the rock above, and splinters rained down like a hailstorm. It went on for about a minute and then it stopped. I could hear someone shouting, "Cease fire! Don't waste your ammunition. Cease fire!"

The side of my face was all bruised from my trying to push down through solid rock, and my knees and elbows ached as if they had been hit with iron pipes. I could feel the rock dust matting my hair, and the backs of my hands were all gray-yellow, and my teeth grated over each other like fine sandpaper.

"Who's that up there?" Barrow yelled. "Freedman. Is that you, Freedman?"

I rolled to my left side and pointed my mouth at the rock above me so I could use it as a sounding board. "Give it up," I yelled. "Give it up, Barrow. We've got people inside the mountain now. We've got you on both sides. Billy Bob is dead. Phil is dead. Your wife is dead. Give it up."

There was a murmur from below, kind of like you hear from the chorus when you go to one of those Greek plays that college drama departments do sometimes. Cathy and I had gone to one once, and sometimes she would imitate the chorus sound after we had made love and she had gone to the bathroom or something and come back all naked. She would float around the room in a kind of a dance where her feet didn't seem to touch the floor, making that noise, that low moan that sounded like the surf at night, and then she would jump on top of me and we would wrestle until she got me all excited again and then she would make a different kind of a moan.

They didn't moan when I mentioned Billy Bob was dead because it caught them by surprise, but by the time I got to Phil and Mrs. Barrow, they were attuned and they moaned.

"I don't believe you," Barrow shouted. "I don't believe you, you Judas, you lying Jew Judas. I don't believe you. Phil is alive. Barbara Barrow is alive. Billy Bob is alive. You couldn't kill them, Jew. You couldn't kill Jesus and you couldn't kill them."

"They're dead, they're all dead," I shouted. "And you'll all be dead too if you don't throw down your weapons and give yourself up to the authorities. Roger is dead too. Don't let any more die. Give yourselves up."

"My baby!" a woman screamed. "Have they killed my baby? Oh, my God. Have they killed my baby?"

That stopped me for a moment. I couldn't start yelling down that her baby was all right. I couldn't retreat from the position I had taken, which was to bullshit the entire congregation into believing that it was all over, that their only recourse was to surrender. I didn't even feel bad about what that mother was going through. She was one of the sons of bitches who had started it all and was down there shooting rock splinters up my ass.

"Revenge," howled Barrow out of nowhere. "We are coming for you, Jew. We are coming to make you pay for every hair of our loved ones' heads. Stand up, everyone, and shoot at the fiend up above, and then come with me into the mountain and help me nail him to the cross of our faith."

The hail of bullets this time was so intense that I thought they'd knock the mountain down behind me and I'd be stranded straight up in the air just like the fox with the roadrunner. I started to wriggle back into the doorway, hoping to get in far enough to cut and run without being hit by a bullet or a rock splinter. And that's what saved my life.

Because just as I had backed to the point where I figured it was safe enough to stand up and run back into the tunnel and try to lose myself somewhere in the maze, they hit.

They were Navy jets from the San Diego base to the south, and I found out afterward there were four of them. It's too bad Moran couldn't have been alive to see it because they were to me what those boats on the river in Vietnam were to him. I had seen pictures on television, in living color as they say, of what napalm can do to an area, but that gave not a billionth of a sense of what that explosion of flame can do. The planes screamed by so fast and so loud that I had no idea what they were, but the four of them carpeted the whole length of that canyon with heat that melted the very surface of the rock. I was quite a ways into the tunnel, which saved my life, because I would have been turned into a cinder if I had stayed on that balcony. The heat was so intense that it sucked all of the air out of the cave for what seemed an eternity, and I could not breathe, I could not move, I could not think. It was about as close to the nuclear holocaust as Barrow could have imagined.

When I finally crawled back out on the terrace and looked down on the little valley below me, there was nothing, not even a scrap of cloth or paper waving in the wind. The log buildings in the rear were still burning, but in moments they too collapsed into the ground. There was nothing, nothing, nothing, nothing at all.

I knew that down below me a lot of people had just been crisped to death, and that some of them had been guilty of nothing more than faith or stupidity, but I couldn't feel anything for them at all. It wasn't just that they had been trying to kill me, that they would have done anything to me that Barrow told them. It was because they were like a disease, a disease that infects everything it touches, and when it is wiped out, the only thing you feel is that a tremendous burden has been taken off your chest and you can breathe deeply again.

I was unable to move from the spot, all energy drained, and when the first police helicopter came flying in some minutes later and drew close enough for me to make out the features of a guy I knew sitting in the copilot seat, I wasn't able to even wave back at him despite the contortions he was going through.

My body knew before my brain that it was all over, that things were about to return to what most people considered normal. All my muscles relaxed, all of them, without exception, and I suddenly had to yank off all the cartridge belts around my body, haul down my pants, and leave my own load right across from the one that Moran had deposited. His had come out of one end and mine the other, but we were both making exactly the same statement about life's little vagaries, and I only hope that someday a graduate student in archaeology from whatever planet is investigating our burnt-out globe comes across the two piles of dust and calls out to his companion, "These creatures were more complex than I thought."

26

There was hell to pay, of course. You just don't napalm American citizens, thirty-seven of them as it turned out, practically a whole goddamned church, without segments of the press, Congress, the ministry, and little old ladies in tennis shoes being angry and distraught in varying degrees.

The problem, of course, was that it was a white church and not one of those radical black offshoots that periodically have to be rooted out, as in Philadelphia and Arizona. The southern press was especially horrified by the crisping of what seemed a bunch of good old boys who wanted nothing more than to preserve all the verities for which their nation stood. The newspapers did acknowledge in paragraphs way down in the stories that it was too bad that four police officers were somehow killed while all of the above was going on, but accidents do happen when people get excited, you know.

The liberal newspapers came up with a mixed bag in which they deplored the actions by both sides. The editorials all concluded that there definitely had not been enough dialogue between the contending parties and that there should have been much more talk before such drastic action was taken. Our local newspaper printed excerpts from editorials throughout the nation and the world, of which I read every word, and the only pundit I agreed with was the one who said you probably had to be there. I was talking to a retired cop at a banquet once and he was telling me about his ordeals as a marine in the Pacific in World War II.

"A lot of people criticized Truman for dropping the nuclear bomb on the Japs," he said, "but as one of the guys who was about to have to wade up on that shore, I thought it was the best move he ever made."

The President of the United States justified his signing of the consent order by saying that all appeals had failed, that four policemen had already been killed and several more were in imminent danger of death at the hands of these fanatics, and that they had established an armed force and insurrection within the boundaries of the continental United States.

I have a feeling that despite his official justification, the President must have had some big second thoughts about the action, because the dropping of napalm while television cameras are grinding away is fairly spectacular stuff, as I can attest to personally. But the government made a big deal about displaying all the church people's weapons and ammunition and uniforms just as President Reagan had done after the Grenada invasion, and the pictures of all that deadly material on television and the front pages of newspapers and the covers of news magazines smothered fairly well the protests of those who decried using American military forces against their own countrymen and deep frying men and women in a canyon cauldron. Who remembers the names of those involved in the Kent State shootings?

How did I feel about it personally? I'm with the old cop who didn't want to banzai the Japanese. Those mothers were about to come into that mountain after me when the blast hit, and if my people had taken time to chat about the situation a bit more, I would have been the fifth police fatality in the official history of the event.

The lucky thing is that all the little kids were still in the room with Felicity and Marianne, and they came through with nothing more than maybe a little diaper rash. Even luckier was that the two dogs, one male and one female, that the Reverend Barrow had allowed in the compound as the breeders for the future, were also unscathed. If even one of those dogs had been singed, the outcry could not have been stilled. You can do whatever the hell you want to people in the United States of America, but you better not fool with the dogs.

Also, the lady and her son whose lives I had spared in the big room were great witnesses to the evils that Barrow and his missus and Phil and Billy Bob had perpetrated. I had a problem making up my mind about the lady and her son once things had quieted down. She had gone as I had told her to the room where the captain and the others were locked in, but then she and the boy had just sat outside the door without opening it. They hadn't done exactly as I had instructed them, but then again she didn't go running to Barrow and they had never hurt anybody. I didn't vote them into the club again, but I did speak a few words in their behalf and they got off with probation.

Fortunately, or unfortunately—I still haven't made up my mind about it and probably never will—Phil and Mrs. Barrow didn't smother under the mattress covers, and I laid everything on them. *Everything!* Including the murder of Mr. Dienben.

If I'd had my way, I would even have cited them for the way their vehicles were parked in the area.

I also told in graphic detail how Mrs. Dienben had twice saved my life and what a credit she was to her adopted country. I kept saying that she and Moran were the heroes in the whole mess, but I could tell that the more I said it, the better I came off. You could see by the looks on the faces of the TV commentators and the newspaper reporters, supposedly the most cynical sons of bitches in the world, that they were seeing through my modesty and self-effacement. When I first noticed it, I started to get mad and I almost reached out and grabbed a TV guy to shake some sense into him. I kept telling myself it was useless to try and convince anybody, but deep down I was worried that this was what I really wanted all the time, that I enjoyed being the lone hero, the survivor, the one who made it through the death camp and lived to tell the tale. Sometimes I wonder who I really am.

They sure made a big fuss over whoever the hell I was supposed to be for a couple of weeks. It first happened when I ran down and around through the tunnels until I came to the one where the lady and her son were sitting outside the captain's cell. When I opened the door and let the whole crew out, they were all over me. Even Schiavone, who didn't make sergeant when I did and had never really said hello to me again after the list was posted, was hugging me and saying what a great buddy I was.

The captain kept trying to shove the five thousand dollars into my hand. The envelope had broken and he had this wad of fifty-dollar bills, a hundred of them, that he insisted I take after he found out we weren't going to have to fight our way out of the place. There were some women and old people still in the mountain in addition to the children, but most of them didn't even know how to use weapons and kept walking around with their hands held up in the air. All of the fighters had been in the canyon and they were gone. Some of them real gone.

I kept telling the captain to hold on to the money, but he insisted I take it. He was intrigued enough to ask me how come somebody like Dwayne Hamilton had brought the cash himself to the station, and I told him the insurance story I had made up for Barrow and he let it go for the moment. But he was cop enough to know that the whole thing sounded fishy, and he knew the kind of business that Hamilton regularly handled as well as I did. Secretaries brought five thousand dollars, not Dwayne Hamilton. But even the captain wasn't going to give me a hard time at that stage of the game. Someday in the future, when he was pissed off at me over something, he might bring it up again, push it a little further. But right then he was happy that his fat ass was still in two pieces, and I was the guy who had unlocked the cell door.

As a matter of fact, everybody gave me just the opposite of a hard time. Much was made of my relentless tracking of the killers of Dienben after my own tragic personal loss; much was made of my coming out of the lion's den and then going right back in to free my buddies; much was made of my battle with the enemy once I had broken loose; and much was made of the fact that I refused to talk more than the minimum about my own exploits except to verify those statements made by my superiors.

I was ordered to take a month off for rest and recuperation, and once the newspapers and television stations realized that I was serious about not making any statements, they mostly left me alone. There would be an occasional call from a free-lance writer who had wangled my unlisted phone number out of somebody, and lots of offers in the mail from people who wanted to collaborate on a book, but silence was always my answer. I didn't want anybody digging in my garden because I didn't really know what might be growing there.

I had dinner at the Doc's house one night, I had dinner with the Dienben children at their place, and I had dinner at Dwayne Hamilton's once, but otherwise I stayed in the apartment and put together little meals for myself from the stuff the cleaning lady bought for me once a week.

The dinner at Doc's was nice. His wife cooked exactly the same meal she had before, which I think was her standard company repast, and they both kept smiling at me. Once in a while Doc would squeeze my shoulder, and when I left, the missus gave me a big hug and a dry little kiss on the cheek. They never mentioned the eighteen thousand dollars, although I could see it was on the tips of their tongues the whole time. Doc was probably building it up as he could, and one day he would hand me a check for the entire amount. Probably over another roast beef dinner.

The meal with the Dienben children was strange, to say the least. I would like to know exactly how many, or rather, how few words were exchanged for the two hours I was there. The older son was obviously the boss now, and he greeted me most formally at the door. He and I sat in the living room having a drink of scotch and soda, without ice, while the girls readied the meal. We then ate several courses in silence except for the son asking me if I would like more and me refusing. The girls never looked up even when they were passing a dish around.

At the end, the brother and I had another scotch and soda in the living room, and then I left. The girls came from the kitchen to bow me out alongside the brother, but even then their faces were tipped just enough to avoid eye contact. I wondered how much they knew of what had really happened, both to their father and between their mother and me, but I realized I would never find out. The meal was the final formality before they dropped the curtain. When I left, I wasn't even sure they would give me a good deal on a car trade.

I called a guy I knew in vice and got Darlene's address from him, and then I packed all of Cathy's clothes in cartons and had them trucked to her place. I went through every pocket and pocketbook and box, but there was nothing more than those original credit cards I had found. I cut up the cards in very small pieces and put them out with the trash.

When I was packing Cathy's clothes, I folded everything as neatly as possible, but I did it quickly so I wouldn't be remembering something we had done when she was wearing this dress or that sweatshirt. I thought of maybe leaving one piece of clothing hanging in the closet, kind of like a memorial, but then I thought of Buchenwald and the Vietnam war wall in Washington and the Bittenberg cemetery and other places like that, and how Cathy would have thought it was a piece of bullshit, so I dumped it all, including the hangers.

I started to throw her jewelry in with the clothes, but then I figured that maybe some of it was expensive rather than the paste I thought it was, and maybe I should have it checked over sometime. A lady who had six million dollars could have bought herself a pair of real diamond earrings. When I realized what was going through my mind, I almost became sick to my stomach. Here I was supposedly mourning my wife and I was thinking in terms of bucks. What the hell was I going to do with the jewelry, real or fake? But then again, why should someone like Darlene get that big a bonus? I dumped it all in one of the bureau drawers as something to be dealt with in the future. The room was finally bare of everything that had belonged to Cathy. Now all I had were pictures and what was inside my mind. They were all I needed.

Darlene obviously got the wrong message from the gift because she was constantly leaving messages in my mailbox, but I never wrote or called her. Once she kept ringing the doorbell, but when I looked through the one-way mirror and saw who it was, I just went back upstairs. I'm pretty sure she was wearing one of Cathy's dresses. A pale green one with what I think they call a yoke neck. Yeah, I'm sure it was one of Cathy's dresses.

Most of the time I just sat in the living room and looked at the wall. I tried watching television and reading books, but about ten minutes was all I could take of any of it. Sometimes I got out the cassettes of my father playing the violin when all his fingers were strong and straight, and I would wonder what I should have done to have been closer to him. And little memories of my mother would push their way in, of things she had said or caresses she had given, and I would feel so guilty about the way I had treated her that my belly would knot up into almost unbearable spasms.

I would sit there and think back on my whole life that I could remember right up to the very breath I was taking at that moment. I would always stop right there, however. I never went into the future. I knew I would have to testify at the trials of Mrs. Barrow and Phil and whoever else the district attorney wanted to send away. I would go over all the details in my mind because I wanted those two to die if possible. I didn't just want them to rot in jail; I wanted them to die. But I wanted them to die only after they sat in jail for a long while knowing they were going to die. The mood in the country had changed. A majority of the people was ready to have criminals die for their sins. Even though I was a cop, I had always waffled when it came to the death penalty. We sometimes made mistakes, and I didn't like thinking about the possibility of an innocent person's life being snuffed out because I had put the wrong pieces of evidence together. The other thing was that once you got the taste of blood in your mouth, the salt made you hungrier for more. I had seen it in criminals and even in a couple of cops, and I worried about a whole country getting the appetite. The Germans had it for a while, and they almost succeeded in wiping out half my bloodline. Now the Protestants in Ireland were working on the other half.

I knew all this, but right then I wanted those two people to die. They had scared me shitless; they had taken something away from my insides; they had looked right through me and known what was going through my mind as well as my intestines. They had to die.

But what about me? I was going to live. For a time anyway. For a full life span maybe. What was I going to do about me? What was I going to testify about me?

If I wanted, I could soon be a lieutenant. The mayor had practically guaranteed it when he spoke to me on the phone. Lieutenant. Captain? Chief? That could occupy a lifetime. Getting there. Being there. Retiring there. I liked being a cop. I liked bringing criminals to justice and seeing that the average citizen didn't get the dirty end of the stick. The only crap you took was from a superior officer; everybody else tried to be nice whether they really wanted to or not.

But I also had six million dollars, and that, too, could buy a lot of nice from people. It had taken me awhile, but I was at last convinced that I was worth six million dollars. And growing every day. When I had dinner at the Hamiltons', I could tell by the way Mrs. Hamilton was looking at me that she knew I had six million dollars. Discreet as he was, client's confidence and all that other bullshit, Dwayne Hamilton had told his wife that my wife had left me six million dollars. She was looking at me as a cop-hero, a guy who carried a gun and had used it, but most of all she was looking at six million dollars. That was the quality that really impressed her.

What about that six million dollars? What did I think of it? What did I want to do with it? Should I quietly dispose of it, maybe give it away to charity, so that I would have to continue in my present way of life, earning my living, being a cop, worrying about when I could afford a new car or where I might go on vacation?

Or I could keep the money and live a very nice life as a cop, able to afford whatever luxuries I wanted as long as I did it in a way that wouldn't excite the curiosity of my friends, neighbors, and whatever authorities might wonder why I was driving a Porsche. That could be a strain; that could be more of a burden than a pleasure.

Or I could quit being a cop and move where people didn't know me and live like a pasha, including a harem if it so moved me. What would it be like at my age to have only three worries—death, taxes, and revolution? Where did I want to go? What did I want to see? What did I want to do? Who did I want to do it with?

I didn't want to do it with anybody. I felt better about myself because there were no thoughts of and no desire for women. The thing with Mrs. Dienben had been an aberration, some kind of freakish thing that had to do with what both she and I were going through. I had looked at Darlene very carefully when she was ringing my bell and tapping her heels outside my door, and her pert face and taut body had done nothing to me. I still had the palm gun that Sergeant Jenny had given me, and she had left a message for me on my phone recorder, but there was no desire to return the gun and take her up on her generous offer.

Although all of Cathy's clothes were gone from the apartment, she was now with me more than ever, and I felt her presence and mourned her loss to the point where I had to interlock my fingers to keep from breaking whatever was within reach. When I was sitting in the living room with a book propped open on my lap and my eyes staring at the wall, I would think about all the things she and I had done when the world looked like forever, and when I was lying in bed at night, I would reach out my hand to the spot where her wasted body had lain and go over every painful moment of the months when she was dying.

I got down on the floor and did fifty pushups and two hundred situps and leg rolls and hydrants and full bends until my body was soaked with sweat. I would do this six or seven times a day when all else failed. Sometimes I would get out of bed and do it in the dark at three or four in the morning, and then take a shower and sleep for a couple of hours and wake up and do it again. I kept asking Dr. Freud what I was trying to sweat out of my body or wash away in the shower, but he never answered. He and Cathy were both dead.

So there I was in the thirty-third year of my life, all alone. Basically, I was once again starting from scratch. The only difference was that this time around I had a hell of a lot of scratch to work with. Somebody in Cathy's family, probably her father, had laid millions of dollars on her and she had passed it on to me. I was upset because she hadn't told me she was terminal when she married me. But then again, she knew all the time that she was going to leave me six million dollars when she died. I felt my heart stir within me as the realization hit. She wasn't being selfish when she did it; she was being the soul of generosity. We had those good months before the bad. She had put no clouds in the sky. There had been no need for a past because my Cathy, my wife, my love, had only been thinking about my future.

I dropped to the floor and started doing push-ups, determined to go for an extra fifty. Then I was going to take a shower, a long shower, and get dressed, duded up even, and go to the best restaurant in town and have a very elaborate meal. With a good wine. A very good wine. Which I would pick according to the price, because I really didn't know a damn thing about good wines.

And I would drink the whole bottle in silent toasts to the lady who had made sure that whatever my future might be, it could afford to be a noble one. I could barely hear the echo of her giggle.

"Benny," she was saying, "Benny, my love, my only. Don Fugaroun."

I started counting out loud as my arms shoved my body in the air and then down again—"Two forty-eight. Two forty-nine. Two hundred and fifty."

I collapsed on the floor, the side of my face buried in the carpet, and I couldn't tell from the noises I was making whether I was laughing or crying.

Whichever it was, the bong of the doorbell shut it off. I looked at the clock and saw that it had to be the mailman. They still had the old custom in our neighborhood of ringing the doorbell after they had shoved the mail in the slot. I didn't even pick up the mail for days until the poor man left me a note saying how tough it was on him when I didn't remove it each day, because there was no room for the new stuff.

I wiped my face roughly on a towel, wrapped the cloth around my neck and went down the stairs. There was nobody visible through the peephole so I opened the door, unlocked the box, and removed the wad of contents. I threw it on the table in the living room and got myself a glass of orange juice, then came back and sorted through it. The junk stuff was thrown in the basket, which left three letters, one from the mayor's office, one from ABC television, and one that had nothing but my name and address. The letter from the mayor had to do with the presentation of a commendation medal in two weeks' time. The one from ABC was an invitation from the host of "Good Morning America" to appear at my convenience and tell my story as I wanted to tell it.

The third one had just a single sheet of paper with two sentences on it, but it made my heart quicken as it hadn't since the napalm had taken the rest of my eyebrows off. The words were typed and centered on the sheet. They said:

> YOU HAVE FIVE MILLION DOLLARS
> THAT BELONG TO US.
> WE WILL BE IN TOUCH.

The words came as a relief and I could feel the tension go out of my body as I read them over and over. There were somebodies out there besides the Trust Department of the Bay City Bank who knew about Cathy and her money. They didn't know that it had grown nearly a million bucks since she had inherited it, but they probably knew who it came from and why. And they would probably know where she came from. Who she was; who she really was. I knew that I was never going to rest easy, that I was never going to make up my mind about what I wanted to do with my life until I knew too. Until I cleared it all, I was never going to be able to have a real relationship with another woman, and I knew damn well that I wanted to, that I didn't want to be alone on a permanent basis, because to be alone was not to be really alive. I wanted to live. Never again. Never again.

I pulled the telephone book to me and flipped the yellow pages to airlines. I wasn't going to wait for whoever was going to "be in touch" to make the first move. The thing to do was visit the Bay City Bank in Upsala, New York, and put the squeeze on Wenker and the Trust Department. It looked like I was going to have to earn the six million dollars the hard way.

What was it my father always said?

"You know what you get for nothing in this

world? *Gornisht*. Nothing. That's what you get for nothing. Nothing."

The Jews have seen it all. But what about the other half of my genes? The leprechauns say go for it.

I wondered what kind of connections you had to make to get to Upsala, New York, up near the Canadian border. I could fly direct to New York City, and then there had to be some feeder airline, or I could rent a car or . . .

What the hell was I thinking about? I was thinking like the old Benny Freedman, the guy who thought ahead to Supersavers and redeye flights and Tuesday specials. The new Benny Freedman, the one who had been reborn in a canyon fire, didn't operate like that. Not him. Never again.

I ran my finger down the page, stopped at what looked like a good one, and dialed the number. It was answered on the first ring.

"Yes," I said, "I want to inquire about chartering one of your executive jets."

About the Author

Milton Bass lives in the hills of western Massachusetts with his wife and youngest offspring. He is the entertainment-travel editor of *The Berkshire Eagle* in Pittsfield, Massachusetts, and is an avid vegetable gardener.